Trains reign supreme.

Every time I go to jump on a steam train as it chugs its way through Rowlesburg—

Every time I throw out my hands to grab the rusty metal rungs and haul myself up onto the side of one of them black coal cars, hoisting my knees up over its churning, screeching wheels—

Every single time I jump on a train—my heart thumps even noisier in my ears than the clanking of the old iron horse I'm hopping up onto. I love steam trains. I love living in a town that's chock-full of 'em. They're as much a part of my life around here as the mountains. Or breathing.

But it's a dangerous business, hopping a ride onto a moving train. First off, there's always a right decent chance of getting killed. Second, and about ten thousand times worse, my father might find out.

But I'm not like Dad—I don't mind breaking the rules now and again.

OTHER BOOKS YOU MAY ENJOY

Al Capone Does My Shirts	Gennifer Choldenko
The Best Bad Luck I Ever Had	Kristin Levine
The Desperado Who Stole Baseball	John H. Ritter
The Last Newspaper Boy in America	Sue Corbett
The Liberation of Gabriel King	K. L. Going
A Long Way from Chicago	Richard Peck
The Schwa Was Here	Neal Shusterman
A Season of Gifts	Richard Peck
Sticks	Joan Bauer
A Year Down Yonder	Richard Peck

WHEN THE WHISTLE BLOWS

FRAN CANNON SLAYTON

PUFFIN BOOKS
An Imprint of Penguin Group (USA) Inc.

Patricia Lee Gauch, Editor

PUFFIN BOOKS
Published by the Penguin Group
Penguin Young Readers Group, 345 Hudson Street, New York, New York 10014, U.S.A.
Penguin Group (Canada), 90 Eglinton Avenue East, Suite 700, Toronto, Ontario, Canada M4P 2Y3
(a division of Pearson Penguin Canada Inc.)
Penguin Books Ltd, 80 Strand, London WC2R 0RL, England
Penguin Ireland, 25 St Stephen's Green, Dublin 2, Ireland (a division of Penguin Books Ltd)
Penguin Group (Australia), 250 Camberwell Road, Camberwell, Victoria 3124, Australia
(a division of Pearson Australia Group Pty Ltd)
Penguin Books India Pvt Ltd, 11 Community Centre,
Panchsheel Park, New Delhi - 110 017, India
Penguin Group (NZ), 67 Apollo Drive, Rosedale, North Shore 0632, New Zealand
(a division of Pearson New Zealand Ltd)
Penguin Books (South Africa) (Pty) Ltd, 24 Sturdee Avenue,
Rosebank, Johannesburg 2196, South Africa

Registered Offices: Penguin Books Ltd, 80 Strand, London WC2R 0RL, England

First published in the United States of America by Philomel Books,
a division of Penguin Young Readers Group, 2009
Published by Puffin Books, a division of Penguin Young Readers Group, 2010

5 7 9 11 13 15 17 16 14 12 10 8 6 4

THE LIBRARY OF CONGRESS HAS CATALOGED THE PHILOMEL BOOKS EDITION AS FOLLOWS:
Slayton, Fran Cannon.
When the whistle blows / Fran Cannon Slayton.
p. cm.
Summary: Jimmy Cannon tells about his life in the 1940s as the son of a
West Virginia railroad man, loving the trains and expecting one day to work
on the railroad like his father and brothers.
ISBN: 978-0-399-25189-4 (hc)
[1. Railroads—Fiction. 2. Family life—West Virginia—Fiction.
3. Country life—West Virginia—Fiction. 4. West Virginia—History—To 1950—Fiction.]
I. Title.
PZ7.S63128Wh 2009 [Fic]—dc22 2008038435

Puffin Books ISBN 978-0-14-241732-4

Printed in the United States of America

Design by Semadar Megged
Text set in Minion

To Dad. And Mom.

And the town of Rowlesburg, West Virginia.

With all my love.

Foreword

I am very fortunate to have a father who told me stories when I was growing up. Dad's stories weren't make-believe; they were about things that really happened when he was a kid, which made them doubly fascinating. He told me tales of death and glory surrounding the Baltimore & Ohio Railroad. And he told me about his father—my grandfather, whom I never met because he died when my dad was just a teen—who was the foreman of the B&O in Rowlesburg in the 1940s. He told me about how he swam in the Cheat River, about the pranks he and his buddies pulled on each other, and about how the dieselization of the railroad led to the decline of his hometown, which had once been so vibrant with life and work and industry.

All these stories noodled around in my brain as I grew up. And my frequent visits to Rowlesburg as a child gave me the chance also to swim in the Cheat, and to listen to the sound of the engines as they chugged their way through town. But I knew the swimming hole I swam in wasn't quite as deep as it had been for my father, and I was hearing the tinny horns of diesels instead of the deep whistles of the old steam engines. As a result, I developed nostalgia for a time and circumstance I'd never known myself, but that I had accessed through my father's memories. And I loved it.

Although this book is set in 1940s Rowlesburg, the events described are fictional, as are its characters. I have, however, named some of the characters after members of my family, in their honor. And a few of the stories were indeed inspired by some of the tales my father shared with me when I was a child.

Fiction has been described as "the lie that tells the truth." Many of the facts and much of the regional history in this book—dieselization, the addition to the M&K Junction, and the shutting down of the Manheim cement plant, for example—are true events, although I have rearranged them at times to serve story over fact. I have found this necessary not only to maintain the narrative structure I've chosen, but also to be able to cut through mere fact to arrive, I hope, at a story that points to an even greater truth.

Fran Cannon Slayton
Charlottesville, Virginia

WHEN THE WHISTLE BLOWS

STEAM TRAINS

Every time I go to jump on a steam train as it chugs its way through Rowlesburg—

Every time I throw out my hands to grab the rusty metal rungs and haul myself up onto the side of one of them black coal cars, hoisting my knees up over its churning, screeching wheels—

Every single time I jump on a train—my heart thumps even noisier in my ears than the clanking of the old iron horse I'm hopping up onto. I love steam trains. I love living in a town that's chock-full of 'em. I love being on 'em, being anywhere near 'em. They're as much a part of my life around here as the mountains. Or breathing.

But it's a dangerous business, hopping a ride onto a moving train. First off, there's always a right decent chance of getting killed. Second, and about ten thousand times worse, my father might find out.

But I'm not like Dad—I don't mind breaking the rules now and again. So, risky as it is, I hop on a train any time I have the chance. Because once I'm on a train, my heartbeat settles down to the steady, pounding rhythm of the tracks, and I know I'm right where I belong. And when I close my eyes and let the rush of wind blow back my hair, I know that like my brother Bill, like my father, my grandfather and all my kinfolk going all the way back to when we Cannons first came over from Ireland—I am going to be a railroader one day.

No matter what Dad says.

My dad's the foreman of the railroad here in Rowlesburg, and he doesn't want me nowhere near the trains. Can you believe that? He says they're a dying breed. Says there's no future in them. But I think he's the one that's the dying breed. The steam trains'll be around forever. But my dad? Well, probably the best way to describe my dad is to say that his birthday is tomorrow. Halloween. Or as he calls it, "All Hallows' Eve." The day of the dead. Or really, the day the dead come back and haunt the living. You know, trick us. Confuse us. Scare the crap out of us.

It's a heck of a day to be born on, really. But I've gotta say that as far as I can tell, it suits Dad pretty durn well. Because you never know what kind of exciting things just might head down the tracks on All Hallows' Eve—besides the trains, I mean.

A MIDNIGHT MEETING

ALL HALLOWS' EVE 1943

The bedroom that me, Mike and Bill share sits only about ten feet back from the railroad tracks that run through Rowlesburg. Every night the trains hit their whistles right outside our window as they crawl through town, shaking every timber in the house and every last one of my ribs right along with them. It's tradition for Baltimore & Ohio Railroad engineers to hit the whistle when they pass by the foreman's house. And since Dad's the B&O foreman, they always go and hit it right by our window. That's how come I learned early on to sleep with my pillow over my head.

But it's the middle of the night, and Mike's snatching the pillow right off my face. Mike's my middle brother. Mike's a pain in the you-know-what.

"Jimmy, get up," he whispers.

I grab at the pillow as he rips the covers off my bed, and I'm on my feet ready to punch him. He's standing there by the door with my quilt in his hand, dressed in his jeans and a coat. I scan the room looking for a little help from our oldest brother, Bill, but his bed is empty. Bill's one of the few boys over eighteen that's not away at war on account of his job on the railroad being so important. Still, I know he's not pulling the graveyard shift over at the M&K Junction this week. Where the heck else could he be this time of night?

"Stop it, you idiot," whispers Mike. "Get yourself dressed. There's something important happening." Before I can even ask what, he flings the pillow at my head and walks out the bedroom door like he owns the whole house.

I catch the pillow just before it hits my face and stare at the empty door frame. He's only three-and-a-half years older than me. Who the heck does he think he is, anyway? Dad?

I drag on my clothes and jacket as fast as I can and hop after him, still pulling up my pants as I reach the bottom of the stairs. He's gotta be bluffing. Nothing important happens this time of night. Nothing in Rowlesburg, at least.

But then I remember—it's All Hallows' Eve! Dad's birthday!

I scramble after Mike through the dark kitchen, making sure to pick up my feet so as not to stumble over Dad's boots by the door. But it turns out I don't need to. Dad's boots aren't there tonight.

I follow Mike outside, rubbing my eyes, trying to get a handle on what the heck could be going on. It's cold out here. The fog's oozing down the sides of the mountains. Typical West Virginia October. But not typical Rowlesburg. I don't think I've ever been outside so late—or so early?—in my whole life. I blink to get my bearings. The town's different this time of night—like a log all hollowed out with dark rot. There are no bunches of us boys kicking the can in the street. No ladies headed towards the five-and-dime, swatting their kids in line behind them. Just lampposts and pavement and fog. Even the echo of the Mallet engine's whistle sounds like a ghost of its daylight self.

Our cat, Amos, yawns at me from the porch, his fangs reflecting the half-moon's light. It *feels* like it's still All Hallows' Eve, but now I'm not so sure. It was when I went to sleep. If you go to sleep and then wake up in the middle of the night, does that make it tomorrow? Or is it still today? I start to ask Mike, but he shushes me, putting his finger up to his lips.

I ignore him. "Is this some kind of Halloween trick?" I say. Loudly.

Mike looks at me like I'm the one who's the pain in

the you-know-what. The town's completely quiet except for my voice and the miles-away *ch-ch-ch-ch* of the last train through, echoing back down the river as it makes its way towards Tunnelton. It'll likely be near about an hour before the next one passes through town, snaking its way through the dark passes in the mountains.

"No, Runt," he whispers. "Ain't no trick."

I scamper forward a few feet to catch up to him. "So d'ya mind telling me where we're going then?"

He puts his finger to his lips again. "Wait 'til we get past Rail's and I'll tell you the whole thing."

I roll my eyes and drop back to follow behind him again. As if he's really got a "whole thing" to tell about.

Rail's is the local grocery, owned by my father's friend Rail Whittle. We both know that Rail is likely as not to be staggering around this time of night. He's a good old guy, but he hits the moonshine pretty hard, and it makes him stay up late and wander the tracks.

The light in the grocery's on, but there's no sign of old Rail himself, so we run past the store towards Tar Hole, the section of town on the other side of the railroad tracks. I don't really understand why they call it Tar Hole, because there's no tar and no hole to speak of, except for where the potholes in the road are all patched up. Come to think of it, there are a lot of potholes in Tar Hole.

We stop running at the edge of the salt lick, panting clouds of cold breath. Mike's words come out and hang like little silver ghosts in the moonlight before the wind comes and steals them away.

"The Society is meeting tonight."

My breath gets stolen, too.

The Society? A pilot light goes on in the back of my head. Whisperings I've heard before. Rumors about men meeting in the dead of night. Of unseen rituals. Secret initiations. My memory kick-starts, recollecting the way me and Mike—and in my earliest memories, even Bill—used to peek down the steps late at night, way after bedtime, watching Dad walk out the kitchen door with a bottle of whiskey in his hand. *Going to a meeting, Mary Etta,* he'd say to Mom. A Society meeting. A meeting us kids weren't supposed to know anything about, much less discuss.

I stare at Mike. I can't believe he just said those words. It must've been a good five years since I've heard them mentioned out loud. *The Society.* Years since the day Dad caught me and Mike pretending like we were going to one of his secret meetings, making believe we were drinking out of that old whiskey bottle we'd found out in the field behind the house. Heck, we were just little kids—I was what, six or seven maybe?

That day floods my mind again, clear as the waters of the Cheat River. I remember Mike pretending he was making some kind of speech. And me right beside him, making believe I was the best machinist on the whole entire railroad, tipping the empty bottle up to my lips, just like my father. We knew durn well Dad didn't want us to know anything about The Society. Or to ever go to work on the railroad, either, for that matter. But we wanted both so daggone bad we could taste it, all sooty like the coal dust that settles each night on the porches of this town, left by the overnight steam engines, swept away again and again every morning.

But that day the kitchen door slammed shut on our daydreams, leaving Dad standing on the porch, staring dead at us. And his granite eyes told us he knew what we were doing. We figured on getting a tanning like we'd never seen before. But he just went back inside the house and never said a word. To us, at least.

Bill was the one who cornered us later that night. He was almost sixteen and had already dropped out of high school to work on the railroad. The Society was nothing but a kids' fairy tale, he told us. It wasn't real. Our pretending had to stop.

We hated giving up our secret game, but we didn't want Dad to get after us. Heck, we'd already seen firsthand how mad he could get when Bill up and quit school. We'd do anything to avoid having that kind of heat be directed at us. So we promised Bill we'd never say another word about The Society ever again. And neither of us ever did.

Until tonight.

I look at Mike. He can't be lying—he wouldn't bring it up again after all these years unless it was true. I wanna believe him. But I can't. This is Mike Cannon. My brother. The pain in my you-know-what. He's gotta be conning me.

"You're lying," I tell him. "Just trying to get me all riled up because it's Halloween."

"No, Jimmy," he says. "The Society's real. And we're gonna see it tonight." The moonlight on his face makes him suddenly seem older than before. "Bill tipped me off on where they're meeting."

"*Bill* told you?" I suck in a cold breath. It feels like a ghost is rising up from the dead inside of me. "Where?"

"Down at the funeral home."

"The funeral home?"

My voice doesn't sound as scared as the knot in my stomach says I am. Seems like the funeral home is the only home our boys in the service have been coming back to lately. Just the mention of the place gives me the heebie-jeebies. I look at Mike, waiting for him to crack a smile and end this stupid joke. But his face looks just as serious as the mountains.

I decide to call his bluff, and start off running towards the funeral home. He grabs me by the arm, pulling me back.

"Jimmy, hold on a second."

I look at his hand gripped tight around my arm and

start to grin. I got him—he's bluffing! I wiggle out of his grip and look him right square in the eyes. I stop grinning. I'm dead wrong. He's biting his lip, and not to hide a smile, either.

"Slow down," he says. Each word comes out in its own private patch of fog. "This ain't kid stuff, Jimmy."

And the way he's looking at me, I suddenly know that it ain't.

Without so much as another word Mike turns on his heel and starts out in the direction of the funeral home. I can't do anything but follow, but there's a squirrelly feeling in the pit of my stomach that follows right along with me.

The wind has picked up and makes a low groaning sound in my ears. As we pass by the darkened houses, I see the remains of jack-o'-lanterns on the porch steps, their triangle eyes melted smooth from the fire that lit their insides just a few hours ago. As we pass, their faces change expression in the shadows, the black of their eyes hollowed out like potholes in the night. I zipper up my jacket to keep the cold out, following in Mike's footsteps exactly so I don't have to think about where I'm heading.

When I finally look up, we're standing in front of the red door of the funeral home.

"How we gonna get in?" I ask. I'm sorta hoping that we can't.

Mike cracks a grin and pulls a thin metal file out of his coat pocket.

"Lemme see." I go to grab it out of his hands, but he pulls away. Too fast. Its tip scrapes the paint, leaving a six-inch gash in the door. I stop grabbing.

"You idiot," he whispers. "You're gonna get us caught."

I back off and he opens the door with the file. Easily. Like he's done it before. I don't ask.

We slip inside, shutting the door fast behind us. The first thing I notice is the dust. It's everywhere. Including up my nose. I hold in a sneeze as we tiptoe towards the back parlor. I'm starting to wonder if we're actually walking through dust or little bits of someone's Great-Aunt Edna.

I follow Mike without asking questions, to make up for the scratch in the door. I don't know what's gonna happen, but I know we've gotta be quiet. We go into a dark side room where Mike sits me down in a dusty upholstered chair. He motions for me to stay put, so I do, watching him go through another door into the only room in the place that's lit. The light coming through the door causes shadows to scuttle across my face and hands, reminding me of the river rats in the shallows of the Cheat. I pull my feet up onto the chair real fast.

Mike comes back in quickly, shuts the door until it's almost closed, and motions me to come over.

"Just keep quiet and watch," he whispers.

I cock my head and stare through the crack in the door. It's pretty shadowy inside, even though the light's on. I squirm for the best view I can get, squished underneath Mike, whose height gives him a better line of sight.

It takes a couple of minutes for my eyes to adjust to the light coming from the room. As they start to focus, I begin to trace the outline of shapes, furniture for the dead. The wooden shelves next to the far door hold tools the likes of which I've never seen before—tools that look like they belong in a really mean dentist's office, all metal and hooked—along with a brush, a comb, and a few dirty-looking needles.

I start to wonder what they use needles for on dead people, when I notice that the gray cement floor is stained with dark red lines that form little paths heading directly down into the drain. *Yikes!* I try to swallow, but all the spit in my mouth is gone.

In the middle of the floor is a huge stone slab. Sitting on it is a big bottle that reads EMBALMING FLUID. But it's not the slab or the fluid that inhales my attention through the crack of the door. It's the pine coffin that's lying open on top of it.

There's a body in it.

My stomach does a double flip. From my spot under Mike's chin, I can just barely get a glimpse of the dead man's face in silhouette. The shape of his nose is incredibly familiar, unmistakably round—a heck of a lot like Dad's. *Holy mackerel!* It only takes about a second for my Adam's apple to swell to the size of a pumpkin. It's not Dad. It's my uncle Dick. How could I have forgotten he'd be here? The crappy feeling I've been trying to forget about for the last couple of days shoots right up to the front of my chest again.

It happened just the day before yesterday. Uncle Dick had been leading a crew as they tried to hoist a derailed steam engine back onto the tracks. It was something he'd done a hundred times before in these mountains—heck, anytime a train goes off the tracks around here, they always call in Uncle Dick instead of having to wait on the big crane out of Cumberland. They had it almost all the way back up on the rails when a cable snapped and the rear wheels slipped, cutting his right leg off several inches above the knee. They couldn't stop the bleeding.

A tear surprises my eyelashes and rolls right down onto my shoe—*thwip*. I jerk my sleeve up to my eye to make it stop, holding my breath, trying to force the pumpkin back down my throat. Dick was my absolute favorite uncle. Heck, he's the one who taught me everything I know about steam engines. Taught me how to fish and hunt, too—Dad was too old to bother by the time I was finally of age. Dick was gonna take me out this November on the first day of hunting season. He said he'd see to it for sure that I'd get me a big buck this year.

Mike puts his hand on my shoulder. I can't tell if it's his hand or my shoulder that's doing the shaking.

Slowly, the far door in the embalming room opens. At first the door frame is empty, then fills one by one with the forms of—*I can't believe it*—it must be The Society! My heart is racing now as each member steps from the darkness into view. First . . . my father! Then Heevie Marauder, Rowlesburg's deputy sheriff. Next comes Old Rail, followed by my mother's brother, Uncle Clarence, who's the high school biology teacher. And then—*holy mackerel*—it's my brother Bill!

The smell of whiskey and snuff fills the room as they gather in a circle around the coffin. Old Rail speaks.

"The Lord giveth. The Lord taketh away. *Benedìctus Deus in Sàecula.*"

"*Benedìctus Deus in Sàecula.*" *Blessed be God, forever.* Automatically my lips make the familiar shape of the words I know so well from Mass, in unison with the men's booming response.

But then I pull my face away from the door. What the heck are they doing? I look up at Mike with a question mark on my face, but he just gives my shoulder a silent squeeze, his eyes staying glued on The Society.

I look back in through the crack and see Uncle Clarence pulling out an ancient brown leather book. He begins flipping through its pages. I've never seen anything quite like it before—the markings inside look like old-fashioned script, the lettering all looped and flowing.

Clarence finds what he's looking for and hands the book over to Bill, who clears his throat and begins to read. The rest of the men bow their heads like they're standing in church.

"'None of us lives to himself, and none of us dies to himself,'" reads Bill. "'For if we live, we live for the Lord, and if we die, we die for the Lord.'"

I can't figure how Uncle Dick's dying would do a daggone thing for the Lord or anybody else, but several grunts of approval from the men echo around the room.

"'Do not weep,'" Bill continues, "'for I shall be more useful to you after my death and I shall help you then more effectively than during my life.'"

I can't help but think of the first day of hunting season without Dick. There's no chance in the world I'll be getting me that buck this year.

I look at the book. It's not a Bible, but what the heck is it? I watch as Uncle Clarence helps Bill close it.

"Hold it up like this, Bill," Clarence says. "Flat."

Bill holds the book flat on top of his palms as Uncle Clarence proceeds to fish out a silver tin of snuff from his coat pocket. He unscrews the tin and pours a pile of the powder out, right onto the cover of the book. He takes a pinch and stuffs it behind his lower lip, then motions for Bill and the others to do the same. When they're done, Clarence blows the rest of the snuff into Uncle Dick's casket.

Now Rail pulls a whiskey bottle from his coat pocket. Up it goes to each pair of lips, slowly making its way around the circle. Finally it reaches Heevie, who closes his eyes as he takes a good, long swig. He wipes his mouth with the back of his hand and starts the circle off, telling stories about Uncle Dick.

"I remember Dick . . . ," each begins.

"The golden gloves champion."

"The hunter."

"The hundred engines he hoisted back onto the tracks." They go around again.

"The night we set the outhouse onto the roof of the church."

"The day he met Aunt Mary." They go around again.

"That day he jumped into the Cheat River to save the Graff boy from drowning." They go around again. And again. And again. I never heard half this stuff before. I knew he was a great uncle, but . . . how come I never *really* knew?

Suddenly, The Society shifts positions so the coffin—so Uncle Dick—becomes part of the circle. My father is on one side. Old Rail is on the other. They lean down and—*Holy Mother Mountain, they really are*—they're lifting Dick's head and shoulders out of the coffin!

Dick's body is straight as a poker as Dad and Rail struggle on either side to haul him partway out of his casket. When they finally get him set up between them, I find myself looking right at Dick's paste-white face. It's Uncle Dick, for sure. But somehow it doesn't look like the real Uncle Dick at all. Or at least the Uncle Dick I thought I knew. The pumpkin in my throat swells to the size of a watermelon. As I wipe my eyes with my sleeve cuff, I hear my father begin to speak.

"Ricky," he says. I look back through the crack. Dad's arm is around Uncle Dick's shoulders, holding him up. And his mouth is right up next to Uncle Dick's ear. Dad's lips are blood red. Uncle Dick's ear looks like white candle wax beside them.

"Ricky," my dad says again. His voice seems like it's about to break in two pieces.

Mike squeezes my shoulder hard, as if it might help squeeze Dad's voice back together. Somehow it does.

"Ricky, you was the cheatin'est son-of-a-gun ever played the game of gin."

The room busts into laughter.

"Sure as heck was," Rail says, slapping Uncle Dick on the shoulder as if he were propped up on a bar stool instead of in his coffin. Dick's stiff body jolts sideways, then snaps back into place.

Mike and I have to chuckle, too. Uncle Dick was the worst cheater at cards in the whole town, and everyone knew it. He always carried extra cards up his sleeve. And it's not like he tried to hide his cheating, either. It was just a little extra rule in the game whenever you played him. Heck, the backs of the cards he carried rarely matched the ones that were being played. He'd slip in a blue-backed king of spades when you were playing with a red deck. If you caught him, he'd just laugh it off and put it back up his sleeve so he could try again later.

The laughter's done good for Dad. He's got a real smile on his face now, looking at Dick. The kind of smile I don't see on him all that much—the kind that sprints down from his eyes and runs around all over his face.

"Heard those angels are pretty tough to beat up there," he says. "We wanted to make sure you was ready for them."

He pulls a blue-backed playing card out of his pants pocket and slips it up Uncle Dick's shirtsleeve.

"It's an ace, Ricky," he whispers.

Thwip. I jerk my sleeve up to my eyes again. It's an ace of hearts.

"You got the other present, don't ya, Rail?" Dad asks.

"Sure do," says Rail. "Got it right here."

Rail pulls out an unopened bottle of Paddy's Irish whiskey and hands it to Heevie, who slips it down in the coffin beside Uncle Dick's left leg.

"When you sit down and have a drink with the Boss Man, you tell him we sent the whiskey, okay?" Dad says. He pulls off his glasses, looks up at the ceiling and wipes his eyes with the back of his sleeve. He puts his glasses back on and finally looks over again at Dick. Looks at him hard.

"I wasn't expecting you to up and die when you did, Ricky. None of us was expecting it, was we, boys?"

Everyone shakes their heads, me and Mike included. It almost looks like Uncle Dick is shaking his head, too, his body swaying slightly between Dad and Rail's arms. Dad looks up at the ceiling again and pauses for a minute, taking in a couple of deep breaths. His white fingers curl tightly around Dick's equally white shirt, pulling the collar slightly off center.

"If I'd-a only knowed it, Ricky . . ." He lets the words out fast. "If I'd-a only knowed . . ." He hangs his head down, leaning into Dick's shoulder. My brother Bill thumps him on the back.

"You couldn't have changed it, Dad. Nobody could've gotten that leg to stop bleeding . . ."

My eyes drop down to the coffin. I can't see below Uncle Dick's pants pockets from where I'm squatting. What do they do with a leg that's been cut clean off like that? Is it in there with him, or will they wrap it up and bury it separately in its own little casket? Or maybe they just throw it out with the trash.

I look back at Dad. He's shaking his head no, twisting his lips to let the words out.

"That's not it, durnit, Bill . . . If I'd-a knowed he was going to die . . . If I'd-a knowed he was going to die . . ." He grabs Uncle Dick by both shoulders, looking him square in the face.

"If I'd-a knowed you was going to die, Ricky, I would've sat down and told you a few things first, durn it." Dad's face is only a few inches away from Dick's. His eyes are wide, angry.

"I woulda told you that you don't need to worry about Mary, Ricky. I'll take care of her like she was my own sister. I swear to you and God I will. Take her in under my own roof. Feed her at my own table."

His voice stops short, but his eyes are busting out of their sockets, jerking back and forth across Dick's face. Back and forth again, looking. Searching. I almost expect Uncle Dick to say something. But he doesn't.

"Good God, Ricky," Dad says. His voice is softer now. "We growed up all those years together. Worked the rails together. Every dagburn day."

Dad's eyes are closed now. I can't believe it. He's crying. My dad is actually crying.

"I woulda told ya . . . I shoulda . . ."

He stops again. Nobody else is looking at him anymore. They've all closed their eyes. But I can't. I just can't. He holds his brother in his arms like he's rocking a baby.

Rail finally opens his eyes, remembering his whiskey. After he takes a swig, he nudges Heevie, who drinks and passes it to Uncle Clarence. After Clarence, it goes to Bill. Bill takes a long draught, then puts his hand on Dad's shoulder. Dad finally opens his eyes and lets go of Dick's body, allowing it to rest again between him and Rail.

"It's time now, Dad," Bill says, gently offering him the bottle.

Dad's hand is shaking as he takes the whiskey and brings it up to his mouth. When he finally pulls it down, he wipes his face with his shirtsleeve, then looks again at Uncle Dick.

"Here's to you, Ricky . . ." His voice crackles.

Dad holds the bottle up to Dick's pale lips, tips Dick's head back and pours the last few sips into his open mouth. The whiskey disappears down Dick's throat.

Dad's steadiness disappears, too. His shoulders begin to shake as he lowers his face towards Uncle Dick's. Their noses are touching now, Dad's wide-open eyes looking down into Dick's closed ones. Dad opens his mouth as if he's going to say something, but no sound comes out. He's wheezing. Hard. Dad's tears are rolling down Uncle Dick's cheeks now. It looks like they're both crying. Dad finally closes his eyes, shaking, and rests his lips on his brother's forehead. The wheezing slows down. Slows down. Stops.

I feel Mike's arms pulling me away from the cracked

door. Tears dripping down my nose, I look up at him half angry, half relieved to have the sight torn from my eyes. I wanna throw a punch, only I don't know who to hit.

"We've gotta go now, Jimmy," he whispers.

I let him lead me away, back through Great-Aunt Edna, back through the scratched red door. My breath becomes visible again as I follow him out into the night. The next train has made its way through the mountain passes and now lets out a single, steaming whistle as it moves slowly through the town. As we turn to follow it home, I hear the bell-like tones of my father's tenor borne up on the wind:

Oh Danny Boy, the pipes, the pipes are calling
From glen to glen, and down the mountainside
The summer's gone, and all the flowers are dying
'Tis you, 'tis you must go and I must bide . . .

I stop and close my eyes, wondering at the sound. I never knew before tonight that my father could even sing.

OF TOMBSTONES AND CABBAGES AND KINGS

ALL HALLOWS' EVE 1944

Dad says every railroad payday brings half a million dollars through this town, and it's without a doubt my favorite day of the month—the one day where pretty much everything happens. On payday, you can always watch the men buying beer at the beer garden, or the ladies walking up to Rail's to get their groceries for the week. Mom'll sometimes sneak me a nickel and me and my buddies'll put our coins together and run up to the five-and-dime to buy kite string or gum or whatever else might strike our fancy. Payday's the day that the hairbrush and fish-oil salesmen always come by and visit Mom, and the neighbor ladies titter and cackle in their backyards, laughing between laundry wires and wet sheets. On payday it feels like Rowlesburg is full and fat and ready to take on anything the world might have to offer it from the trains that move the wartime cargo east and west across these mountains.

And today is a once-in-a-blue moon payday because it's also Dad's birthday—he's sixty-three today. Which of course also means it's All Hallows' Eve. A triple whammy! I can't wait until tonight when me and my Platoon of buddies are gonna get together and figure out all kinds of tricks and treats to scare up around town. We'll have this place turned upside down by the time we get through!

But the biggest trick of all will be making sure Dad doesn't find out what we're up to.

Right now Dad and I are on our way to the gas station, ration cards in hand, for his idea of a big treat—picking up his favorite pipe tobacco. But as we cross the street, Stubby Mars suddenly squeals around the corner and yells at me out the window of his '41 Buick.

"Twick or tweat, wittle Jimmy! You dwessin' up as a fuzzy-wuzzy bunny wabbit tonight?"

I grit my teeth and glare at him. Stubby is my brother Mike's best friend, and he's just as much a pain in the you-know-what as Mike is. The two of them are forever taking digs at me and my Platoon buddies. But it's gotten downright intolerable since Stubby got his new car last month. They think they're a couple of real big shots now.

Well, they'd better watch their step if they know what's good for them.

Stubby's car is midnight blue and in disgustingly perfect shape, which of course is the whole reason why he's yelling at me—to make me look at it. I gotta admit it's a beaut, with a huge sloping hood that could easily hold up under a German grenade attack. I mean, it's a monster. A looker, too.

Cars are more than just a pastime to Rowlesburg High School upperclassmen; they're a living, breathing, oil-changing obsession. I can see Stubby and Mike laughing in the rearview mirror as the car squeals away. Pains in my you-know-what, the both of them.

I spit hard onto the ground. The spit is good quality—heavy and thick with no lumps—and it comes out in a perfect, spinning wad that slaps itself onto the ground just the way I'd like to slap Stubby upside the head.

My father snorts. He doesn't look at Stubby's car. He doesn't look at me. He just looks straight ahead and snorts, without missing a step. What the heck is a snort supposed to mean? Is he laughing at what Stubby said? Or is he poking fun at the way I spit? There's no way of knowing with Dad. But either way it makes me mad. I clamp my teeth together and look straight ahead, catching sight of Heevie Marauder and little Thaddeus Ore waxing Heevie's car at the Esso station on the corner of Buffalo Street.

"Happy birthday, W. P.," Heevie hollers at my father as we walk up to them. "How's it feel to be thirty-nine for the twenty-fourth time?"

My father snorts again, this time with a half smile. I clench my fists. Why can't he just skip the snort and go directly to speaking, like everyone else?

"Beats the alternative, Heevie."

"I guess."

Dad nods to Thaddy and goes inside the station to get his tobacco. I stay outside, leaning against a telephone pole and daydreaming about tonight, punching the side of my fists into my legs to make the time somehow go faster. I can't wait!

Heevie grunts hello to me and goes back to waxing his car—another '41 Buick. He's always waxing his car at the station on his day off. He's almost as old as Dad, but he's still just as obsessed with cars as the high school boys. Seems to me like a man his age ought to have graduated from cars to trains by now, but not Heevie. Maybe it's got something to do with him being deputy sheriff of Rowlesburg—he's always chasing after cars and people, not trains. With few exceptions—my father and Thaddy Ore are two—he doesn't seem to like people as much as he likes cars. Leastwise kids. But I guess you can't spit-shine a kid as well as you can a car.

No wonder Heevie and Dad get along.

Heevie's round circles of wax streak bright in the sun,

then mellow to a sheen on the black paint as he buffs them out. I look over at Thaddy, who's turned his circles into smiling faces, first buffing out the mouths, then the noses, leaving all the eyes for last. Thaddy's own eyes flutter over in Heevie's direction, making sure he's not looking; then he bends down and gives a short, quick wave to each waxy eye before rubbing it gently out with his rag.

Thaddy's probably a good thirty-five years old, but ever since I can remember, he hasn't been right in the head. There's always been different stories as to how he got that way. My buddy Red Hezz swears a tree fell and hit him on the head so hard that it sunk him straight down into the ground up to his knees. Says they had to pluck him up out of the dirt like they was pulling up a radish. But Bill says it was Thaddy's older brother that beat him upside the head with a gooseneck wrench so hard it left him half blind and nearly dead. Either way, Thaddy was working at the M&K for Dad about the time it happened. They say he was a heck of a machinist beforehand, but he's never been worth a counterfeit dollar ever after. Dad still keeps him on at the shop, though, even though Thaddy can't do anything but light cleanup work now. He lives over in the beat-up old boxcar that sits at the edge of the train yard.

That's it—the train yard! Maybe the train yard would be a good place for me and the Platoon to stir things up tonight. Only trouble is, if we go anywhere near the train yard, there's a good chance a railroader might see me and tell my father what I was up to. Nah, better stay away from the yard tonight.

Dad finally comes out of the station, his pipe already lit. The smoke rises in little puffs around his head like a miniature steam engine. He nods good-bye to Thaddy and Heevie as we start walking the long block back to our house. Just as we're passing St. Philomena's a flurry of bicycles speeds by us, heading past the gas station. It's my whole Platoon, pedaling fast to Tar Hole. Neil Fisher's at the front, and he yells back at me to follow.

"Come *on*, Jimmy!"

Something's up—the Platoon is meeting early. I look up at my father, who gives yet another snort. I roll my eyes, figuring he must mean it's okay for me to go. I bolt to the house, grab my bike and pedal hard towards Tar Hole. I know where they're going; it's where the Platoon always meets on that side of town—the cemetery.

Finally, we're gonna hatch our plan for tonight! But why so early? My heart knocks at the inside of my chest, hurrying me to pedal faster. As I round the corner, I can just now see the cemetery coming into view at the end of the street. The tombstones stick up sharp out of the dirt, standing like an army of ghosts at the edge of town.

The cemetery's the oldest part of Rowlesburg, going all the way back to 1858, when the town was first founded. Some of the graves are so crumbly now that the names on them are pretty much unreadable, except maybe by the dead man's kin. It's where my uncle Dick was buried last year, along with practically all my other relatives going all the way back to when us Cannons first came over from Ireland and started working on the railroad. It's off the beaten path, and is pretty much the perfect place to scare up a little trouble any time of year.

I catch sight of my Platoon sitting on the old stone fence at the edge of the cemetery. The branches of the trees are swaying hard in the wind, bending low to the ground as if they're gonna pluck one of them right off the fence and send him sailing high up into the air like a train whistle.

I kick my bike off into the grass beside the fence. My usual place is there waiting for me between Neil Fisher and Mulepile Wilson. I sit down facing the tombstones, trying to figure out why everyone's suddenly in such a hurry. Neil's talking, leaves are blowing, and I can see by the look on everybody's face that they've got their ridges up.

". . . so obviously he's been at it again for the past two days straight. Who else here's had it happen to them?"

Four out of the seven boys put their hands up. Everyone groans.

"See, that's just not right. Enough's enough. He's gotta be stopped this time, that's all there is to it."

"What's not right?" I ask.

"It's Stubby Mars," Neil says. "He's been at it again in that stupid new car of his—half the time with *your* brother, Jimmy. Yellin' crap out the window. Even ran Red Hezz and Ajax right off the road when they were minding their own business just riding their bikes. All told, he's got six of us one way or another in the past two days."

"Make that seven," I say.

Another groan breaks out among the tombstones, then quiets so I can tell my story about Stubby and his shiny Buick. When I finish, everyone starts talking and groaning and yelling about Stubby all at once. There are lots of words flying around at odd angles. Something's gotta be done. And it's gotta be done tonight. We're seeing red, that's for sure. Then, out of nowhere, Neil's wearing it.

Phwap! The front of Neil's T-shirt is suddenly dripping red. It looks like he's been shot! We all stand looking at him for a moment, frozen.

Phwap! Phwap! Mulepile and Ralphie Botch are the next hit, one on the head, the other on the knee. *Thwuh, thwuh, thwuh!* I duck down behind the fence as a barrage of color flies over my head.

"What the . . . ?"

I look over at where the flying objects are now lying splattered on the ground. Tomatoes. Rotten tomatoes.

While we'd all been griping about Stubby, we violated rule number one of Platoon meetings—always post a lookout.

The rest of the Platoon scrambles for cover behind the nearest tombstone. I hear fits of laughter coming from the road. I peek over the fence to get a look, but I already know who it is.

"Twick or tweat, wittle felwas!" hollers Stubby, leaning out the window of the perfect Buick. He's wiping his hands with a yellow and black bandana as he and Mike and their two other buddies squeal away, their faces red only from laughing so hard.

I turn back to the cemetery to assess the damage. I've never seen a sorrier-looking Platoon. I'm the only one who hasn't been hit. Everyone else is wet and red from hair to socks. It'd be a funny sight if I was looking at another Platoon. But it's us.

Red Hezz hangs his dripping red head and starts walking towards his bike.

"Where you goin'?" I ask.

"Home," he says. "No reason to stay out here wearin' rotten tomatoes, is there?" He picks some of the rot out of his hair and throws it to the ground.

I sit back down on the fence in my usual spot, careful not to sit on any of the tomato pulp. A couple of the other guys begin to straddle their bikes, carefully wiping the juice off their handlebar grips as an engine blows its whistle from across the river.

"Now hold on a second here," I say. "We're not just going to roll over and let him get away with this, are we?"

Red Hezz looks down at his bicycle pedals. Mulepile shrugs his shoulders. Somebody halfheartedly mutters "no."

"Well, I'm not," I say loudly.

Red Hezz looks up at me for a second, then goes back to his bike pedals. We're standing at the crossroads of Platoon history. It's either defeat or revenge. I hawk up a juicy one and spit it into the dirt.

"Neil," I start out, "all this time we been planning to scare us up some kind of big trouble tonight—and here's our perfect chance! You ain't just gonna let it pass us by, are you? You ain't just gonna let Red Hezz get smacked upside the head with a bunch of tomato rot and not do anything about it, are you?"

Neil looks over at Red Hezz, who, despite his best efforts, still has tomato seeds plastered to his forehead.

"Ain't Red Hezz your buddy?" I ask Neil.

Neil grins. "Yeah, he's my buddy." Red Hezz looks up again, letting a smile leak out of his mouth.

"Ain't Red Hezz the one always gives you a smoke when he gets 'em from his old man?" I ask.

"Sure is," says Neil, looking over in appreciation at Red Hezz.

"How 'bout you, Ajax?" I ask. "Ain't Neil and Mulepile your buddies?"

"Sure they are, Jimmy. You know I wouldn't-a made it through the seventh grade if it hadn't-a been for them letting me copy."

"Right. So you gonna just stand by and let Stubby Mars make them look like a couple of fools?"

"No!"

"No's right!" I shout. "How's about the rest of you? We're buddies, ain't we?"

"Yeah!"

"And we're not just buddies—we're the Platoon, ain't we?"

"Yeah!!"

"And Platoon buddies stick up for each other—right?"

"RIGHT!"

"Okay, then! Meet me back here at eight o'clock to defend the honor of this Platoon!"

Cheers go up as if we're already avenged. Everyone gets on their bikes and rides off towards home. Everyone but Neil Fisher.

"Okay, ol' Platoon buddy, what's the plan?"

"I'll 'splain you the whole thing when we meet back here at eight, Neil."

"So you don't have one then."

I look over at him. "Right."

Neil grins and shakes his head. He starts slowly pedaling back towards the other side of town, but stops after a few feet and turns around.

"Meetcha back here a half hour early," he says.

I decide to walk my bike back through Tar Hole to give me some time to come up with a plan. I watch the spokes of my tires going round and round, dry at first, then splattering with mud as I come to the edge of the old salt-lick field. There are other tire marks here. Car tires.

Of course. That's where Stubby got the tomatoes. The Victory Gardens.

The Victory Gardens for the war effort take up every last clod of dirt in the old salt-lick field. It's really the railroad's land, but they let everyone in town use it to grow food since the war broke out. In the summertime, beefsteak tomato plants compete for position with carrots, cucumbers, corn, you-name-it—if Burpee has a seed for it, you can find it growing here. It's a perfect place to grab a tomato off the vine and eat it like an apple on the walk home from the swimming hole. But by the end of October the field is like it is today—mostly just bare and brown. Even the cold-weather crops like cabbage and lettuce are rotting.

I grab one of the tomatoes off its dead vine and throw it in a high, long arc towards the river. It falls way short and lands with a splat, making me want to spit another good one upside Stubby's head. I call up a wad from way in the back of my throat and plant it a couple of feet away, right on top of a rotting cabbage. If the cabbage was Stubby's head, the spit would've landed squarely in his left eye. I picture Stubby blinded by the sticky wad, running his Buick off the road into a ditch. That'd work. But how am I gonna get close enough to spit through his window? I'd have to be as close as I am to . . . the cabbage . . .

I go over and pull the head up by the roots. It's perfect! It's heavy with rot, but the roots are still firmly attached, giving it a sturdy sort of handle. I swing it over my head, laugh out loud and fling it towards the river. It sails over the spot where the tomato had landed and drops right at the edge of the water's sandy bank. I've got my plan!

By the time the whole Platoon gets back to the cemetery, it's pitch dark. Neil and I have already pulled up every last rotten cabbage out of The Gardens and stacked them high behind the stone fence like a pile of cannonballs. They're practically as heavy as cannonballs, too. Frozen almost solid.

"He'll never know what hit him!" Red Hezz says, laughing as he picks up one of the cabbages and lets it fly into the darkness of the graveyard.

"Don't waste 'em on the dead folk," says Neil. "We got a live one to git!"

I don't have to tell them the plan. When Stubby drives by, we're gonna plaster him and Mike with cabbages. Simple. Easy. Beautiful. Then we're gonna run like mad dogs!

The only thing we've gotta wait on now is for Stubby to drive by. That won't be a hard order on Halloween night, when every kid in Rowlesburg is out tricking or treating or working on some kind of sneaky combination of the two. It's a command performance for every automobiled high school boy to show off his wheels. We'll find Stubby, that's for sure. It's just a matter of time.

And place. The one place everyone drives by on Halloween—the cemetery. It's deadly dark, which'll give us great cover until the last possible minute.

"Here's the plan, men," I tell them. "Neil, Mulepile and Ajax are gonna be the lookouts, see. The rest of us are gonna stay here in the cemetery, and when they give us the signal—plow! Stubby's done for!"

"The usual signal, Jimmy?" Ajax asks.

"Yup, Ajax. The usual."

The usual signal is the *Eeeerrerret* screech. We've been using it since the first day of Mrs. Carmel's second-grade class. You make a high sound way in the back of your throat, drop it down a tone in the middle and then end it in a high-pitched question mark. We think it sounds like a bobcat. Dad says it sounds like a platoon of eighth-grade boys that's up to something.

Ajax's eyes flash excitement. "Okay, but I wanna carry a cabbage with me to the lookout post," he says.

I roll my eyes. "Don't you think it would look sort of suspicious if someone sees you carrying a rotten cabbage down the street, Ajax?"

"Not on Halloween."

"Even on Halloween, Ajax." Mulepile and I try to explain why, but it's just not getting through.

"I don't care," Ajax says. "I'm taking one with me. I'll pretend I'm dressed up like the Headless Horseman, like what I copied from you at school, Neil."

I shake my head and look over at Neil for some help, but Neil just shrugs and grins.

"Okay, Ajax," Neil says. "You can take *one*, but you have to lay it on the ground when we get to the lookout post. Deal?"

"Deal."

"Okay," I say. "No more questions? Good. This is Operation Halloween Revenge. Every man to his post!"

Ajax, Neil and Mulepile head up the street. The rest of us decide to move the cabbages behind the first row of tombstones so we have something extra to hide behind while we're throwing them. As we gather them up, we look into the cemetery and hesitate. It's so daggone dark in there. I can't even begin to see the first row of grave markers.

"Come on, men," I say, trying to sound confident.

"Pair up with the man beside you and we'll hunker down two to a tombstone."

We all look at each other one more time, then step side by side into the complete blackness of the cemetery. When I turn to look back at the street, I can still clearly see the outlines of Neil, Mulepile and Ajax as they head to the lookout post. But here in the cemetery I can't even begin to make out Red Hezz's shape rustling just a couple feet away from me. At least, I *think* it's Red Hezz that's doing the rustling.

I start thinking about all the dead people I'm walking over and become distinctly aware of my heart lying inside my chest, suddenly kicking upwards like it wants to come right out my throat. I stretch one hand out in front of me against the dark, my fingers searching for a tombstone. It seems like I should have reached one by now. My ears suddenly prick up to all the sounds around me: the shifting of weight, the crunching of leaves, but most especially the frosty silence that drapes itself around us all like the white cloth on top of a coffin.

My hand finally hits the tombstone it's been searching for, and it's cold as a block of salted ice. Red Hezz and I settle down behind it, and I try to shift my attention from the rustling noises to the cabbages. My fingers search for a root-handle, sliding through the icy ooze of its rot. I stick my tongue out and try hard not to imagine

I'm touching something that's come up out of the grave beneath me.

Almost immediately a car down the street honks its horn and I hear Ajax speaking to someone—someone with a deep voice. I ready my cabbage to throw, but no signal comes. I peek my head around the tombstone and see a '42 Chevy crawling down the street. It creeps by the cemetery, slow enough for me to make out the silhouette of the driver's face. It's Mr. Pike, the ancient principal of the high school, well known for his uncanny ability to find students in places where they're not supposed to be. We hold our breath. His eyes search the graveyard as we watch him from our perfect darkness, invisible.

"He was lookin' mighty hard this way, Jimmy," says Red Hezz after the car passes from sight.

I drop my cabbage and head out to the street, hopping the graveyard fence. When I get to the lookout post, there is Ajax, standing on the corner in plain view of anyone who might come driving down the street. So that's why Mr. Pike was going so slow.

"You can't let anyone see you, Ajax!" I yell as I run over to him. "Do you wanna get us caught?"

"I told him to duck down behind the bushes with me and Mulepile, but he wouldn't listen, Jimmy," says Neil.

Ajax puts his hands on his hips. "How we gonna get

Stubby to drive by you guys if he don't see us and take the bait?" he asks.

"He'll drive by us, Ajax," I tell him. "Everybody drives by here on Halloween. Just get down and get ready to give the signal when he comes. And don't let anyone see you this time."

Ajax hunkers down in a huff. I run back to the grave markers and whisper what happened to the rest of the Platoon.

Just as I finish, we hear Ajax giving the signal.

"*EEEERRERRET!!?*"

I peek around the tombstone—it's the '41 Buick!

"It's Stubby!" I whisper to the Platoon. "Hold your fire until my word!"

Instantly my palms are covered in sweat. I grip the cabbage root like a handle, cock my arm and summon everything I have inside to keep from throwing it too soon. I've gotta see the look on his face! The car's headlights glare down the street. The muscles in my arms twitch. The car is getting closer, but I still can't see his face. Red Hezz jabs his elbow into my ribs.

"Call it, Jimmy," he whispers.

I shake my head and wait a little longer to get a glimpse of Stubby's eyes. Red Hezz jabs me again. I still can't see Stubby's face.

Another jab.

"Fire!" I holler.

A barrage of cabbages catapults towards the Buick's hood. Directly behind it, I can see Neil's shadow heading towards the cemetery.

Thump! Thump! Splat! The windshield cracks. I bite my lip. Didn't mean for *that* to happen, exactly. Neil's shadow is waving its arms. Why is he coming back?

"Round two!" I holler again, and another shower of cabbages flies, leaving the car's side mirror broken half-way off as they bounce to the ground.

Stubby jumps out of the car in a frenzy.

"I'm gonna wring every one of your fan-dam necks when I get my hands on you!" comes the voice.

But it's not Stubby's.

"Holy Mother Mountain!" My eyes pop bright like a flashbulb.

We've ambushed Deputy Heevie Marauder!

"Run like the river!" someone shouts.

Heevie comes in a tornado towards us, throwing off every cuss word I've ever heard and then some. My feet root into the grave beneath me and I crouch down behind the tombstone, covered by the cemetery's blackness. Red Hezz and the others take off through the darkness towards the river. I should follow them, but my feet won't move.

"I'm gonna kill every last one of you kids!" Heevie hollers, following Red Hezz to the edge of the cemetery, where the bank drops down to a steep snarl of trees that eventually leads down to the river. But they're too far ahead of him.

I look to run north, or maybe west up towards Buffalo Street, but either route takes me straight through the glare of the Buick's headlights. And as much as I want them to, my feet refuse to take me deeper in among the graves.

I look out at the street. The car looks like it's run through a hail of anvils. The windshield is a giant spiderweb, the antenna is clean busted off at the middle and the hood looks like a crater on the face of the moon.

Holy mackerel. Doing that to a cop car is *definitely* against the rules. There's no use in escaping if Heevie sees me. I'll be as dead as the guy under this tombstone the minute he tells my father. And he *will* tell my father.

Heevie's blocking the only dark way out—towards the river. After a minute he gives up on catching the others, turns around, and steps back into the headlights' beam, slowly walking towards me. His footsteps are weighted and deliberate. I hold my breath, barely peeking one eye to the side of the grave marker. Maybe he'll think everyone's gone.

"I know at least one of you's still in there," he says, heading straight towards my headstone.

How can he know? But this is Heevie Marauder, the deputy sheriff of Rowlesburg. He's been chasing the town's kids for coming up on three decades. Of course he knows. And he's gonna tell Dad. My stomach flips. I'm done for.

"Now, where would I be hiding if I was the last one left?" he says, clearly more for my benefit than his own. He's less than five yards away from me now, standing just beyond the stone fence. I close my eyes for a second, trying to concentrate on not moving. But with my eyes closed I lose my balance, catching myself just as my coat brushes up against the tombstone. I pray Heevie didn't hear.

"Heh, heh, heh. I knew you was in there."

I open my eyes and see his figure step from the light of his headlights, over the fence into the graveyard's shadow. The shadow seems to lose its darkness now with both of us in it. He comes closer, still laughing. I crouch lower, holding my breath. He's practically suffocating my poor gravestone now. I hear his coat rattling against the words engraved on its other side. He leans over, reaching for me. I duck my head under my arms. I can smell the snuff in his mouth.

"I gotcha now, don't I, boy?" he says. "This'll be the last time you mess with ol' Heev—"

CRASH! The rear windshield of the Buick explodes into pieces, cutting Heevie's name in half. He turns like a whip and thunders to his car. I look over his head and see two shadows running up the street. It's Neil and Ajax, and Heevie is hot on their tails. Before I can think, my feet are hauling me towards the tree-tangled riverbank.

I can still hear Heevie hollering. His voice is getting farther away, then louder again. It doesn't sound good. When I get to the trees, I hightail it out of the graveyard and head north for a block. I'm home free now—all I've gotta do is keep on running, step through the front door of our house like nothing happened, and Dad will never be the wiser.

Who the heck am I trying to fool? If Neil and Ajax had left when they had the chance, I'd be strung up in the back of Heevie's car right now. I gotta go back. Dad or no Dad.

I circle back in the direction of Heevie's voice to find them. Neil catapults out of the darkness, practically knocking me over. I grab his shirt to steady myself as Ajax scurries into the both of us. They stare at me for a second like deer in the headlights, their eyes stretched wide as four cake pans.

"We can't shake him," Neil pants, trying to disentangle himself. "Run!"

Ajax is blowing some hard wind as he follows Neil towards Buffalo Street. Looking back, I see Heevie's outline moving fast towards us, only about thirty feet away. I grab Ajax and Neil both by the back of their collars and pull them off the street into Bigger Carrico's yard.

"This way," I whisper.

But it's no good. Heevie's still right behind us. We shoot through the yard and clamber lickety-split over Bigger's back fence. We've gained a few steps on him, but even so, Heevie just won't be shaked. And Ajax is slowing way down. By the sound of his breathing, I know he can't go much longer. I look over at Neil.

"If one goes down, we all go down, Neil."

Neil nods. Ajax is looking over at me with panicked eyes. He's starting to slow.

"Just a little farther, Ajax," I say, slowing my pace to stay with him.

"I can't . . ."

"We're almost there!"

"Almost where?"

"The river."

He just about stops right there, but Neil and I grab his arms and drag him forward. We just have to get past the funeral home and cross the Goff property and we'll be in the river. I look back. Heevie's regained the ground he'd lost in the Carricos' backyard. He does better in the flats.

I redirect us towards another fence. Neil practically throws Ajax over it, then picks him up on the other side as we scramble towards the back of the funeral home. It's a good move. It takes Heevie some serious effort to get over that second fence, but once he finally clears it, he's madder than a cinched bull. He busts into a sprint as we haul Ajax down the hill towards the river. At the bank Ajax trips on a root and falls to his knees beside me. I look back, see Heevie charging and haul Ajax up over my shoulder. Neil grabs us both, and the three of us tumble into the dark river.

We gasp at the cold as we slosh our way into the coal-black current. Heevie's silhouette arrives on the bank, heaving and ho-ing and cussing like a hot engine. We bury ourselves up to our eyeballs in the water, holding our breath and listening for the splash of his steps coming into the river. There's no way Ajax can outswim him if he follows us.

We watch him on the edge of the shore, stamping his feet and shaking his fists in the air like he's getting ready to fight the Cheat. He sputters and steams, cusses and swears, but he doesn't set foot into the water.

Ajax lets out a bubbly sigh. Neil slaps me hard on the shoulder. I just close my eyes and grin.

The freezing water weighs down our clothes, but our hearts float high in the current, arms linked as we cross the river side by side. It'll take hours for our clothes to drip-dry as we sit and talk on the bridge, but we don't mind. We've got no place to go. We've got nothing but time. It'd be okay by me if this night just went on and on forever.

And my father will never know.

LAST DAY OF FIRST DAY

ALL HALLOWS' EVE 1945

Dad says it's the first time in West Virginia history that the first day of deer hunting season is falling the day after All Hallows' Eve. Not that having First Day practically be *on* his birthday is any big deal to Dad. He's never been a real hunter. He couldn't care less how Mr. Evans is screwing it all up for the rest of us.

If Uncle Dick was still alive, he'd understand. And he'd do something about it, too. Uncle Dick knew how exciting it is to sit out in the woods at dawn with the train whistles echoing up the sides of the mountains and your backside practically freezing off, just waiting for a big old deer to come by. Heck, as far as I'm concerned first day of deer hunting season is the most important day of the whole entire year, excepting VE and VJ Day, of course. And it's not just me that thinks so, either. It's practically a federal holiday around here—schools across the entire state are *always* closed on First Day. It's just a plain fact.

I don't care what Dad says.

There's good reason for school to be closed on First Day, too, beyond the fact that any self-respecting West Virginia boy wouldn't be caught dead anywhere but in the woods that day. A heck of a lot of folks rely on deer meat to make it through the winter in these parts, especially them that live down in the hollers. Once it snows heavy there, they can't get out until the first spring thaw. And if they don't get their meat early on in the season, they sometimes don't get any at all. Makes for a heck of a long winter of cornmeal mush. And this year, the Farmer's Almanac is calling for the worst winter on record, which is why the governor moved up the first day of hunting season three weeks early this year. What with the war finally being over and all, I reckon he figures there oughta be some deer meat in every pot.

All this makes perfect sense to pretty much everyone in the state of West Virginia, excepting for Mr. Evans, the new Rowlesburg High School principal. He's gone and declared that Rowlesburg High is gonna be open on First Day this year. I don't know who the heck the man thinks he is. Everyone in all of Rowlesburg is ready to run him out of town on a rail.

Everyone but Dad, of course.

Mr. Evans came to Rowlesburg direct from New York City, and he thinks hunting is what he calls "savage." Us kids think he's what we call "an idiot." Lonnie Brice, who's been in the tenth grade for the last three years, called him a daggone Yankee to his face in the hallway just yesterday. Lonnie got a three-day suspension for that little bit of protest. So then Wigger Bowles did the same thing, and he got a three-day suspension, too. It wasn't until Mr. Evans had suspended about ten other boys that he finally figured out that he'd been suspending them all so they wouldn't have to be in school tomorrow, which is the first day of hunting season. Of course that's exactly what they'd wanted in the first place, so Mr. Evans had to back up and cancel every last one of their suspensions. Dad says they got all kinds of sense in New York City excepting the common kind.

Coach Hainsworth even canceled our football practice today because of it. He told us that him and the rest of the teachers were gonna corner Mr. Evans one last time to try to make him give up his out-of-towner plans. Heck, Coach doesn't want to miss First Day any more than we do. It seems like the war's still going on around here. Vertie Gray said her daddy had the daggone mayor here at school during third period this morning trying to talk some sense into the man, but he still wouldn't change his mind.

Meanwhile, here in ninth-grade English class Mr. DeWitt keeps jabbering on about diagramming sentences like First Day doesn't matter at all. But I've decided I'm going hunting tomorrow come heck or high river. And I'm not the only one who's made that decision, either. Not by a long shot.

"Daddy says Saul don't have to go to school tomorrow," Vertie whispers across the aisle to Betty Marire. "It don't make no matter what Mr. New York City says." She pauses to make sure Mr. DeWitt is still facing the blackboard. "Daddy says I can stay home, too, since otherwise it ain't fair."

Mr. DeWitt turns around and furrows his eyebrows at Vertie, who smiles and bats her eyes at him. He goes back to his sentence diagram on the blackboard.

Betty shakes her head back and forth. "Then you and Saul are gonna get yourselves in trouble, Vertie."

Vertie shrugs her shoulders. "Not at my house we're not."

I roll my eyes out of jealousy. It'd have to be the end of the world before Dad would even think about letting me skip school—and even then I'm not so sure he actually would. Ever since Mike up and quit school this year to go work on the railroad, Mom and Dad both have been hammering it into me that I'm gonna be the first in the family to finish high school.

But shoot, I don't wanna finish school. I wanna work

on the railroad like both my brothers. But Dad says he'll flat out kill me if he sees me hanging around the railroad yard anymore. And I figure he'll do the same when he finds out I'm planning on being in the woods tomorrow.

But I'm gonna be there anyway.

The bell rings, jarring everybody in the classroom. It's only halfway through last period, so the bell has no business ringing now. We all look at Mr. DeWitt, who leaves his diagram and walks out into the hallway to find out what's going on. The class erupts into conversation.

I turn around backwards in my desk to face Betty. "I agree with Vertie's daddy," I tell her. "It's not gonna hurt anybody if the whole school is absent for one dag-gone day."

The corners of Betty's mouth turn down. "Well, I'm not missing school, Jim Cannon. I'll be right here tomorrow." Betty's got the best grades at the whole school. She's a stickler for rules, too. Just like Dad.

"Then I'll bet it's just gonna be you and Mr. DeWitt," Vertie says, laughing.

"Heck no," I say, laughing back. The classroom goes quiet. Everyone's listening to me now. "You think Mr. DeWitt's gonna be here on the first day of hunting season? I bet you dollars to doughnuts he calls in sick tomorrow."

I'm expecting a huge laugh, but everyone is quiet.

"Come on, who wants to bet?"

There are a couple of stifled chuckles. Vertie's eyebrows look like they're getting ready to fly off her forehead. She jerks her head towards the door.

"*I* will bet you, Mr. Cannon." It's Mr. DeWitt.

I turn back around in my desk and sink down into my seat.

Mr. DeWitt looks over his half-moon glasses at me and clears his throat. "The rest of you will be interested to know that in five minutes there will be an assembly in the gym addressing Mr. Evans's resplendent views on the first day of hunting season. Mr. Cannon, you will remain in the classroom for a moment while the rest of the class files out in an orderly manner."

Vertie shuffles past me with her eyebrows still bobbing up and down. Betty smirks and does the second-grade shame-on-you sign with her pointer fingers. Finally, I'm left sitting alone in the room with Mr. DeWitt. It's just him, me and the half-finished diagram on the blackboard.

"So, I take it you are going to be in the woods tomorrow, are you, Jimmy?"

I nod. "Yes, sir. That's my plan, sir."

"Well, Jimmy, I am not a betting man, myself. I believe that betting is a poor substitute for actually playing the game. But if I were you, Jimmy, and if I *were* to bet"—he tips his head slightly towards me, raising one eyebrow—"I would bet that I, too, shall be in the woods tomorrow."

A little smile cracks Mr. DeWitt's face. He's a West Virginia boy, even if he does talk sort of funny and insist on carving up his sentences into verbs and nouns. He sends me off with a nod towards the door. I laugh out loud and hop up out of my seat. "Yes, sir, Mr. DeWitt, sir!"

I'm halfway out the doorway when I hear his voice call after me. "Oh and Jimmy . . ."

I pop my head back into the classroom. "Yes, Mr. DeWitt?"

"No one here at school need know that I will not actually be at home in bed tomorrow nursing a sinus infection. Do you understand what I mean, Mr. Cannon?"

"Yes, sir, Mr. DeWitt!"

By the time I run downstairs and into the gym, the whole school is already there. I sit cross-legged on the floor next to Ajax, who tells me rumors are flying that Mr. Evans is actually going to close school tomorrow after all. Can it possibly be true? I look up at the line of teachers leaning against the stage behind the podium, hoping to find a clue on their faces. I catch sight of my uncle Clarence, our biology teacher and my mother's younger brother. He's a hunter, and a daggone good one, too. He's the one who's been taking me out on First Day every year since Uncle Dick died. Heck, he's a big part of the reason I got me that little doe last year. The arms of his tweed jacket are crossed firmly over his narrow chest as he watches Mr. Evans taking the podium.

Mr. Evans is a little rat of a man with a gray suit and round glasses.

"Ah-hem. Testing, testing one-two-three." He taps the microphone several times. "Can everyone hear me?"

We all groan that we can.

"Good. Students, I've called this assembly this afternoon because I know there's been a great deal of hallway discussion about my decision whether to close school tomorrow for the beginning of deer hunting season."

The auditorium swirls with a mixture of hope and hisses. I'm one of the hissers—he said the words *deer hunting* like they're some sort of cuss words.

Mr. Evans scowls at the noise and pounds the podium several times.

"We will have none of that, do you hear me? None of that!"

My buddy Ajax repeats the words *none of that* in a terrific imitation of Mr. Evans's whiny little voice. The half of the school that hears him busts out laughing.

"Quiet!" he shouts. His voice boomerangs around the far back corners of the auditorium, cutting down our laughter. He clears his throat again, and the scowl on his face fades into a fake smile that means the same thing as a scowl.

"School will be open tomorrow."

The hisses start up again in earnest now, this time along with boos and jeers. If he thinks anyone will actually be here tomorrow, the man's gotta be crazy. But Mr. Evans's smile stays starched onto his face.

"School *will* be open tomorrow." Everyone is just plain booing him now, some of the teachers included. He pounds the podium so fast and hard, it reminds me of my aunt Mary's Chihuahua, Lady, scratching for fleas.

"You listen to me right now." The fake smile is still there, but his voice has taken on the low tone of a threat. Our booing dwindles to a murmur.

"There is a little thing we in the civilized world call 'progress,'" he says through gritted teeth. "And like it or not I am bringing it to this little hick town of yours." Even the murmurs have died away now.

The veins in Mr. Evans's temples are protruding like little mountain ranges on the sides of his head. "Any student who does not come to school tomorrow will NOT be suspended," he says.

There is silence. I look over at Ajax, wondering what the heck could possibly be coming next.

"Any student who does not come to school tomorrow," he goes on, "will fail the entire academic year and will be required to repeat his current grade next fall." He leers at us over his glasses. "In other words, you'll be expelled."

It's like the air has been sucked right out of the room. The teachers are all looking at each other. Most of the students' mouths are hanging wide open. After a minute

Ajax finally breaks the silence by coughing out the word *idiot.*

Then Vertie Gray suddenly yells out from the back of the auditorium, "You can't do that!" Her voice bounces around the room like a brave little ping-pong ball before falling silent to the ground.

Mr. Evans's lips stretch around his teeth into an even bigger fake smile, which immediately drops into a sneer. "Watch me."

He swaggers away from the podium, taking steps that are too big by half for a rat his size, and walks out the door. No one else moves.

Finally, my uncle Clarence steps up to the microphone. His round cheeks are as red as the flies' eyes in his biology lab. "This assembly . . ." He pauses, shaking with anger. "This *dagburn* assembly . . . is dismissed." Several boys let out whoops and whistles, but most of us are too shocked to say anything at all. As far as I'm concerned, *progress* is just another word for screwing up things that are perfectly fine just the way they are.

As I shuffle out of the auditorium, it sinks in that Mr. Evans has just upped the ante on me. Dad would've whooped me a good one if I'd gotten myself suspended for one measly day. I hate to think what he's gonna do if I go and get myself expelled for the whole entire year.

I don't care. There's no way in the world I'm gonna

let a rat the likes of Mr. Evans keep me from going hunting tomorrow. No way in the world.

I grab my flannel shirt out of my locker and run outside. Maybe I can find Bill. Or even Mike. They're both hunters. Maybe they can help me think of something.

I fly up the street, hoping to track them down over at the M&K. But I stop short at the corner of Main Street when I catch sight of Uncle Clarence's Chevy. It's sitting in our driveway.

What the heck is he doing at our house?

I hang a quick right at Rail's store to find out. As I come upon the porch, I can see Uncle Clarence through the open kitchen window, flailing his arms, pacing back and forth in front of my father. Dad's sitting at the dinette set, coughing, home from work early again, sick. I sneak my way up the steps onto the porch and listen in.

Uncle Clarence is complaining to Dad about the school assembly! Why the heck is he wasting his breath? He knows Dad doesn't give a rat's backside about First Day.

"I know you've never been much of a hunter, W. P.," he says, "but this is Preston County, not the durn U-nited Nations. Evans has taken this thing way too far. Let me take Jimmy with me into the woods tomorrow morning. First Day means almost as much as the dagburn railroad to him. I'll get him back to school before the last bell rings so they can't count him absent."

Holy mackerel! Uncle Clarence is gonna get his head handed to him.

My father thumps the table hard and lets out a snort. "No, Clarence," he shouts. "The boy can't go skipping school. For God's sake, rules are rules. And he's got to learn they apply to him just like they do to everyone else."

Dad lets out another snort and leans forward towards Uncle Clarence. "But getting back to what you said about Evans—"

Dad's sentence is cut short by a holler from my brother Mike. He's sauntering down the tracks towards our house. "What are you doing sneaking around on the porch like that, Jimmy?" he yells.

Mike almost never comes by the house since the big knock-down-drag-out he and Dad had over him dropping out of school to go to work on the railroad earlier this year. After he moved himself out of the house, him and Dad wouldn't hardly say a word to each other for near a full month. I've only noticed in the last week or so that things between them have begun to thaw a little. So what the heck is he doing coming by here in the middle of a shift? I put my finger up to my lips to hush Mike. But it's too late. Uncle Clarence's head is popping out the screen door.

"Sneaking around, are you?" he says to me.

"No, sir," I say. "Just getting home from school, sir."

Uncle Clarence is practically every kid's favorite teacher at school. He's got a way of making biology halfway interesting, even to the likes of me. But he's no pushover. He eyes me suspiciously. I try to look as angelic as possible, which probably only gets me to looking purgatory-ish, but fortunately it's enough for Uncle Clarence. His eyes fall off me onto Mike. "You're looking mighty strapping these days, Mike. Knocking around under the engines all day must be sitting pretty well with you," he says as he holds the door open for us to go inside.

Dad snorts.

I wince, looking over at Mike to see what he'll do. The railroad's still an awful sore topic between them. Dad told Mike not to go and get a job there. He said the diesels were coming and the engines were getting ready to change. Said the railroad would never be the same. Men were gonna be laid off; the furloughs were already coming, and Mike would just wind up getting let go in a year or two. But of course Mike went ahead and got himself hired on as a machinist anyway. And I don't blame him one single bit. I would've done the exact same thing if I was just a couple years older.

Mike's eyes flash towards Dad for a second, but he lets it pass. "Bill's stuck under that little Mikado engine," he says as he sits down. "Said he'll be along soon as he can." He looks back over at Dad. "So what's got you so fired up it couldn't wait 'til after we got off work?"

I grab a big hunk of Mom's fresh-baked bread off the table and try hard to fade into the wallpaper. Something's going on, and I wanna know what it is.

Dad stays quiet, but Uncle Clarence looks over and chuckles. "We were just talking about—"

But Dad suddenly clears his throat and gives his head a little jerk in my direction. I look back down at my bread, pretending it's a thousand times more interesting than their conversation.

"Oh, gotcha," says Uncle Clarence.

I look up real quick at Dad. He's staring at me. So are Mike and Clarence.

"What?" I say. Dad's eyebrows are raised, like he's expecting me to say something. I know they're not going to let me stay and hear whatever it is they're getting ready to talk about, so I just go ahead and blurt it out. "Why can't I go hunting with Uncle Clarence tomorrow?"

Dad lowers his eyebrows and pushes up from the table. "Well, Jimmy, for someone who wasn't eavesdropping you sure know a powerful lot about what Uncle Clarence and I were just discussing."

I'm caught. He comes over and snatches my ear. "Ow!" I yell as he pulls me towards the door.

"I ought to pull the dagburn thing right off your head just to teach you a lesson," he says, though he lets go of it with a little pat once I'm out the door. "Now get out of here. Your brother and Clarence and I have a few things we need to discuss. In *private*."

He shoots me a long hard stare and then slams the door shut between us. Mike's laughter rings through the window. I rub at my ear and walk down the alley by the tracks, heading towards the back of Rail's store. Where does he get off throwing me out of the house? I'm no little kid anymore. What the heck could be so secret that Mike can hear it but I can't?

I punch my fist hard into my hand over and over again and am halfway to Rail's store when I turn on my heel and decide to head back to the house. I'll be a dag-gone warty hog before I let myself get cut out of this one. I'll find out what the heck is going on. Somehow.

As soon as I get in view of the house again, I see Mike and Uncle Clarence standing on the porch talking and nodding, each with a piece of Mom's bread in their hands. They talk for near about five minutes before Clarence gets in his car and speeds away.

I watch Mike as he turns and moseys down the street, his head tossed back, laughing. I wanna run up and beat the tar out of him to make him tell me what he and Uncle Clarence were going on about, but my head stops me. He's still a right good bit bigger than I am. Maybe better to play the spy instead.

So I follow him.

He heads straight down Main Street, still laughing to himself as he chaws on his hunk of bread. He hangs a right onto Buffalo, then another right straight into Rail's store. I follow him as far as the glass front door and then peek inside. Over by the checkout counter Mike is motioning Rail into the corner. Rail walks over and Mike whispers something in his ear.

Rail scowls for a minute, then gets all disgusted and makes like he's going to spit out his snuff. He glances at the floor and thinks better of it. Mike whispers some more. Slowly, Rail's lips curl into a smile around his yellow teeth. His shoulders shake up and down and his head bobs in a hard nod. He's laughing.

What on God's green earth is everyone laughing at today? Don't they realize First Day is about to be taken away? And nobody seems to give a durn about it except for Uncle Clarence.

Without warning Mike turns his head towards the front of the store. I jump away from the glass door and scamper fast around the corner of the building, squatting down behind a pile of feedbags. I don't think he saw me. But I'm not sure. I peek my head back around the corner. No one's there.

A couple of minutes go by and I finally make up my mind to march back over to the door and just go right in and find out once and for all what's going on. But all of a sudden out of nowhere I'm jerked backwards off my feet, right onto my can! Someone behind me is pulling a burlap feedbag down over my eyes.

"Get off me!" I yell.

But they don't. I try wrenching myself away, but now I'm on my back pinned to the ground with the bag completely over my head. Somebody's kneeling on my shoulders. The somebody grabs the bag along with a right good chunk of my hair and rips both of them off my head.

"Trick or treat!"

Mike is staring down at me, grinning. If my arms weren't pinned, I'd slap that grin right off his face.

"That oughtta teach you to eavesdrop, right, Rail?" he says. I look back over my head and see Rail's face poking out around the back corner of the store. He chuckles as he spits out his snuff and walks back inside.

Mike finally lets me up. "You'll never learn, Jimmy," he says as he brushes himself off.

He may be a full-fledged railroader now, but he's still a humongous pain in the you-know-what.

"Well, if I never learn, it'll be because no one ever tells me a daggone thing," I say as I get to my feet.

Mike laughs, which makes me even madder.

"You tell me what you and Uncle Clarence were talking about," I say, "or I'll . . ."

He smirks. "Or you'll what, Runt?"

"Or I'll . . ." I try to think of something that will really stick in his craw. "Or I'll just have to follow you around until I find out for myself."

Mike rolls his eyes and starts to walk away. I follow behind him, right on his heels.

He turns around. "Oh no you don't."

"Oh yes I do." It's my turn to grin. "Trick or treat yourself."

He rolls his eyes again, like I'm the one who's the pain in the you-know-what.

"Look, twerp. I'll give you one hint, and then you bug off. No more following me and no more questions. Deal?"

I look at him, trying to decide whether to take the offer. It's not like I found out anything by following him to Rail's anyway. I guess a hint is better than nothing at all.

"Okay, deal." Probably a crappy deal.

"The Society is meeting tonight. Twelve midnight. Outside the high school." His eyes are like sparks.

I start to ask all the questions that are busting up through my throat. Why are they meeting? Will Dad be there, too? And how come Mike suddenly knows all this secret stuff, anyway?

But Mike shushes me before I can get the first question out of my mouth. I let myself be shushed. A deal is a deal.

He turns on his boot heel and walks towards the

tracks. After a few paces his voice comes back to me over his shoulder. "Don't let anyone see you there."

I come in early from scaring the grade-school trick-or-treaters with my Platoon over by the cemetery and head straight up to my bedroom. I gotta make sure I'm over at the high school early to find out exactly what's going on. And I've gotta make sure no one sees me.

My bedroom door is cracked as I lie on my bed listening to the shallow coughs and wheezes coming from my parents' bedroom down the hall. Dad had a case of pneumonia late last spring, and the dry heat of summer was hard on him. But now that the weather has turned colder, he seems to be improving again. At least he's missing fewer days of work this month than during the last few.

I listen hard to the sound of Dad's breathing. He's sound asleep for sure, and I suddenly realize there's no way the old man's gonna wake up and head over to the high school tonight. He probably doesn't even know about the meeting. Heck, if I know Mike, he was probably conning me about the whole thing, just to get me off his back. Still, I listen for Dad's footsteps going down the stairs, just in case. Whatever happens or doesn't happen at the school tonight, I'm gonna be there to find out.

I close my eyes just for a moment, but Dad's footsteps never come. When I roll over, I'm dreaming that I'm walking down the hall with Uncle Clarence to the principal's office. Mr. Evans is at the end of the hall with that snarl on his face, tapping the edge of a ruler into the palm of his hand.

Next thing I know, my pillow is over my head and a train whistle is blowing outside my bedroom window. I spring out of bed and into the hallway, telling myself there's no way I could have slept so long. But in my gut I know I'm wrong. The hall clock says—

No. It can't be! Three o'clock?

I've missed the whole durn thing!

I leap down the steps and fly out the kitchen door, lunging back just in time to catch it before it slams shut behind me. The last thing I need to do is wake Mom and Dad. But I'm in too much of a hurry now to be very careful. I break out into a dead run down the middle of Main Street, splashing through puddles left by a late-night rain shower.

When I'm almost to the corner of Buffalo Street, my head catches up with my feet and I slow down. If anyone actually *did* have a meeting tonight, they could be anywhere around here. I may have missed the whole durn thing, but I'll be caught dead before I let Mike know that. I've gotta keep myself out of sight.

And then I hear it—the sound of men's voices coming from the river side of the school building. They're still there!

I retrace my path so I can sneak up on them without

being seen, running behind the home ec building and across the River Road into the wet grass of Riverside Park. I tiptoe over to the park sign and lie down behind it, catty-corner from where they're standing on the school's front steps. The leaves on the ground are wet underneath me, but the bushes around the sign ought to keep me completely out of sight. I belly-crawl my way up to the front bush. Between the branches I can see them standing in a cluster at the top of the steps.

I push some of the leaves out of my face and can just make out the forms of The Society, standing in the shadow of the school—Uncle Clarence, Rail, Bill, Heevie Marauder. And sure enough, there's my brother Mike, too! They must've gone and let him join The Society this year.

Their shadows shift around, and suddenly a white shock of hair jumps out from behind them. You've gotta be kidding me. It's Dad! I can't believe it! And not only is he out here, but he also seems to be pretty much in charge, barking out orders to everyone else.

I hear muffled clanking sounds coming from where the bunch of them are standing. And behind them I see something dark that I can't quite make out from beneath my bush.

My father suddenly turns to Mike and Bill. "You boys go run and get . . ." The rest of his words are carried away by a howl of wind.

Mike and Bill laugh, then grab a hand truck and start wheeling it straight towards me. My sphincter tightens as they charge at my sign. I lie completely still, remembering Mike's warning not to be seen. But they're not coming for me. They pass right by, heading for the ball field on the far side of the park. I watch them as far as my eyes can focus in the dark, wondering what Dad sent them to get.

I look back over towards the school. With Mike and Bill out of the way I have a clearer view of the front door—or what *used* to be the front door. I can't believe what's there now instead—a humongous pile of railroad ties! There must be a hundred of them stacked up there, completely burying the entrance. There's no way in the world anyone'll be getting to within ten feet of that door tomorrow, much less inside.

My eyes shoot over the rest of the building. Every single first-floor window's all boarded up, too! Dad and the rest of them make their way down the front steps, slapping each other on the back and admiring their handiwork. Heck, they must've been at it since midnight. And it'll take hours—if not days—to take it all down again. Let me tell you, nobody'll be getting into *that* school on the first day of hunting season this year!

But they're not even done yet! I hear a scraping sound coming from the direction of the football field. Heevie, Dad, Clarence and Rail walk right by me towards the sound. A minute later they come back into sight, helping Mike and Bill carry one of the huge sleds we use on the football team to practice throwing our blocks.

I lie with my chin in the dirt, completely still under my bush as they bring it down the street, wheeling the thing less than two feet in front of my eyes. I could swear Heevie just did a double-take in my direction. I hold my breath. Thank God his side of the sled suddenly wings around and sends him scampering to keep it on the dolly. I swear that man has seven senses.

Somehow they manage to get the sled balanced again and take it across the street around the left-hand corner of the school, beyond my sight. I hightail it from out of my bushes and hide behind a giant white oak tree so I can see better. They've gotten the sled all the way to the side door of the school. As they slide it off the dolly, it lands with a thud, square up against the door. It'll take more than a fistful of teachers to move that thing out of the way tomorrow!

My dad sits down on the railing by the side door. Even from this distance I can hear him wheezing. The night air is good for his lungs, but the heavy lifting can't be. Bill tells him to stay put while the rest of them go get the other sled. There's only one more door to barricade on the other side of the school, and then the whole entire building will be all sealed up.

As the rest of The Society drags the dolly past the

Riverside Park sign, I see Heevie peer into the bushes again, giving them a little kick. Good thing I moved.

While everyone else is over by the field, my father walks back around to the front door of the school. His wheezing gets louder. He pauses, then sits down on the front steps. Is he all right? Suddenly, he clutches his chest with one hand and leans forward over his knees. The old man's about to have a heart attack!

I'm fixing to run over to him when I suddenly realize he's not just wheezing—he's laughing. And he's not just laughing—he's laughing his backside off! He leans sideways and looks up at the school, then slaps his knee so hard he starts to cough and sputter again.

If I hadn't-a seen it with my own eyes, I would'a never have believed it. He's flat out broken every rule in the book. And he didn't just break them—heck, he busted 'em clean wide open!

By this time, the others have gotten the second sled over to the Riverside Park sign and are heading towards the other side of the building. Heevie kicks again at the bushes under the sign, then looks around and catches sight of my father trying to catch his breath.

"You boys take it from here," Heevie says, running over to Dad.

When he finally figures out that Dad's laughing instead of wheezing himself to death, Heevie gets to laughing himself. The two of them slap each other on the back and walk out of my sight around the corner, meeting the others on the far side of the building.

I step out from behind the oak and am just about to run back over to my spot under the park's sign when Heevie pops back around the corner of the building. He crosses the road and walks right up to my old hiding place in the bushes. I inch my way slowly back around the trunk of the oak so as to be totally out of his sight again. But now I can feel his eyes come to rest on my tree.

I hear Heevie chuckling as his footsteps come closer. The knot in my gut is all too familiar. I stand frozen behind the tree, looking for a way to escape.

"I gotcha now, don't I, boy?" The words ring like an echo in my ears.

His boots take five more steps towards me—*clod, clod, clod, clod, clod*—and he stops. His jacket is rustling just around the other side of the tree.

"Go on and get yourself into the woods now, Jimmy, 'fore your mama gets up," he says. "I don't reckon they'll be having school today."

I hear his feet pivot on the wet grass, his footsteps getting farther away, crossing the street back to the school. I peek my head out from around the tree. He turns around and looks back at me.

"Let's hope you're as good a shot with a rifle as you are with a cabbage."

THE CHAMPIONSHIP GAME

ALL HALLOWS' EVE 1946

The last bell of the day is about to ring and I'm sitting on the edge of my chair, ready to bolt out the door. I'm starting middle linebacker in tonight's championship football game. If we win, we'll not only be Preston County champions—we'll also have the first undefeated season in Rowlesburg High School history. Ever.

Dad says there's no way we're gonna do it, but I know different.

The bell rings, and Neil Fisher and I are out the door.

Mr. DeWitt's voice trails behind us, "Do us proud tonight, boys."

In the hallway, it's a zoo of well-wishers. I bob and weave my way through the backslaps and freshman girls who bat their eyes at me. I hardly notice. I'm on a mission.

I break free of the school walls and meet the rest of the team on the corner of Buffalo and Main. A big helper engine lets off a giant huff of steam at the crossing as we begin our pre-game ritual—what we've done every week since the beginning of the season. None of us will admit it, but we're all pretty superstitious about the whole thing—especially today, on All Hallows' Eve. I mean, why risk losing?

Colored leaves whip off the mountainsides and blow down the wide street, crunching under our high-tops as we walk over to Rail's store, where Rail's got seventeen chocolate milk shakes waiting for us. As usual, Rail's let me off work tonight for the game. And I know when pay-day comes, he'll pay me as if I'd been at the store instead of on the football field.

"I got a lot of greenbacks riding on tonight's game, boys," he says. "I know you won't let me down."

"No, sir!" I say as the others hoot and holler. "Kingwood's only six and four for the season, Rail. We'll have them beat in the first quarter."

"Don't get ahead of yourself there, Jimmy. They may only be six and four, but you know as well as I do they were state champions last year. They got one heck of a good running back. And when a team's got that kind of back, you can never count them out. Especially with your knee still all banged up from last week. Boy, they sure knocked the living snot outta you that day."

"Yes, sir," I say.

My knee. I got hit hard and twisted the heck out of it last week in the game against Masontown. Had to be carried off the field in the fourth quarter. Everyone, including me, wondered all week long whether I'd even be playing today. Doc Arnley had me keep it elevated with ice all last weekend, and by Monday I was up and walking with it wrapped to keep it stable. Every day it's felt better, but I wasn't able to practice up until yesterday, and even then Coach had me keep it real light.

"Jimmy's knee's as good as new," says Corduroy Mars, Stubby's younger brother, who's our senior quarterback. "Ain't that right, Jimmy?"

"It's as good as it's gonna get," I say. "And that's good enough for me to smear the sap out of that scrawny little Kingwood back."

My teammates whoop it up again, but Rail's serious now. "You protect that knee tonight, Jimmy. We made it by Masontown with you out in the fourth, but it could be a whole different story tonight against the Stags."

"Aw, Rail, you're starting to sound just like Dad."

The whooping stops. Everyone looks at me. "Come on, men," I say, downing the rest of my milk shake and slamming my empty cup down on the counter. "I expect it's about time to go pay ol' W. P. our regular pre-game visit. After all, it *is* the old man's birthday."

The rest of the team slams their cups down, too, and we all thank Rail as we file out the door. Like before every other game this season, we're on our way to see ol' W. P.—William Patrick. My father.

The summer was rough on Dad this year—he had another horrible case of pneumonia that's only now starting to get better. And the doctor told him he had to stop smoking because he's got the emphysema. He did stop when he was at home, partly because Mom would have nagged the man out of him if he hadn't. Made him more crotchety than ever. But I know for a fact he was still smoking at work. Whenever he was able to work, that is.

By the end of summer when football practice started, Dad couldn't hardly be around the trains at all. Heck, he could hardly even breathe when he was just sitting dead still on the porch with the garden hose in his hand, spraying the alley down to keep the dust at bay. It was on a hot day like that in early fall that we had our first scrimmage. Coach had sent us on a warmup run through the town, which is how the whole team wound up running by my father sitting out on our front porch.

"You think a bunch of rubber-band-legged boys like you's going to win a single game this season?" he wheezed.

Mom darted back inside to avoid what was coming next. I ground my heels in the dirt and the rest of the team stopped right behind me. I was hot under the collar. Dad or no Dad, I wasn't gonna stand for anybody talking about my team that way.

"You just watch us," I told him. "'Cause we're gonna win the whole daggone kit and caboodle this year."

His snarled eyebrows jutted down over his eyes. "I'll just watch you, all right. I'll watch you get your rear ends handed to you by Tunnelton today."

"With all due respect, Mr. Cannon," said Neil, "the only rear ends gonna get handed anywhere today is Tunnelton's."

We all cheered and started off running again, but not before we heard Dad croak after us, "We'll see what kind of tune you're hummin' after the game today."

Of course after we'd beat Tunnelton in the scrimmage, we all ran back over to my father to tell him how wrong he was. He was still sitting on the porch, holding the hose.

"Well, we'll see what happens when you play your first real game, boys, now won't we?"

I couldn't believe how durn ornery and blind one man could be, even if he was my father.

Anyhow, that's how the whole thing began. And before every daggone game this season we've gone over and listened to him tell us we weren't gonna win! And every single week, after winning every single game, we've gone back and rubbed his nose in it. And then he proceeds to tell us how we're gonna lose the next week.

Well, we're gonna shut the old man's trap once and for all today.

We hang a right out Rail's door and another right into the alleyway that runs alongside the tracks to my house. Before we've gone fifty yards, we can see my father sitting in his usual place on the porch, our cat, Amos, all curled up on his lap—almost like he's waiting on us. My heart beats faster the closer we get. It'll be worth all the grief he's given us this season just to hear him own up tonight about how daggone wrong he's been.

As we get closer, we see his chin is skimming his chest. He's asleep. We all march up to demand our audience with him. But none of us quite has the courage to wake him. We look at each other. A full thirty seconds goes by, and we're still just standing there.

Finally, Corduroy nudges me forward. "He's *your* dad, Jimmy, you wake him."

It's not something I care to do. "You wake him yourself if you want to talk to him so daggone bad," I whisper.

"Who wants to talk to me so daggone bad?" says Dad. He's still got his eyes closed, but his fingers are now scratching Amos behind the ears.

I nod at Corduroy, for him to talk.

"Uh, the football team, Mr. Cannon," he says.

Dad opens his eyes and snorts. "Football team?" he says. "I don't see any football team. Just a bunch of durn lucky country boys is all I see." He closes his eyes again. "Wake me when the football team gets here."

"We're only undefeated for the whole season, Mr. Cannon," says Art Bishop.

Dad's eyes snap open again. "No, Art. *Undefeated* means you've won every game. You've got one game left today. And you're going to lose it."

"Heck if we are, Mr. Cannon," says Art.

Dad props himself up on the arm of his chair and leans towards us. His sudden change of position sends Amos bounding off his lap onto the porch.

"Boys, let me set you straight here today. There has never been a team from Rowlesburg to go undefeated. We're a little train town. You go to a little mountain school. You're little league boys compared to the men over there on that Kingwood city team."

Neil pipes up. "Kingwood's only six and four this season, Mr. Cannon."

"Is that so, Neil?" says my father.

"That's so, Mr. Cannon," says Neil. "*Now* who do you say's got the men on their team?"

"Well, we'll just find that out this evening, won't we? *Boys.*"

We all grumble and turn to go. As we head down the

alley, Dad calls after me. "Jimmy, you take care of that knee."

I don't answer. I'll show him who's right tonight, bad knee or no.

"You hear me, Jimmy?" he says.

"Yes, sir," I say. But I don't turn back. I hear him, that's for sure. But that doesn't mean I've gotta listen.

When we walk into the visitors' locker room at Kingwood High, our conversation goes silent as we look around. It's huge. There are rows and rows of shiny new lockers lining the walls. Matching silver benches are screwed right into the black and silver painted cement floor. There's a Nehi machine in the back corner and a fancy-looking scale on the far wall.

"You'd think we were playing in the durn NFL," whispers Nobe Jenkins.

Heck, until the end of last year Rowlesburg High didn't even have locker rooms for the home team, much less for visitors. We used to just change in the boys' room at school. I don't even know where the visiting team used to get dressed. In their cars, I guess.

Coach looks around and sees our faces. "Don't let the way their locker room looks make you forget the way their record looks." His voice echoes around the empty lockers. "Nehi machines and pretty paint don't make the team, boys."

"Yeah," says Art Bishop. He hops up on one of the benches and plants his fists on his hips. "Who's the team with the best record in Preston County this year, men?"

"Rowlesburg!" we all yell.

That breaks the ice. We unshoulder our bags and start to get dressed out.

"Hey, Grover," says Neil. "That's a cup, not a noseguard."

Grover throws one of his cleats right past Neil's head, but he's smiling. "You watch it, Neil, or I'm-a gonna bust you one."

Grover comes from one of those families that used to get frozen in for the winter down in the hollers. Then a couple of years ago Grover's daddy moved the whole family to town after he bought the Riverside Bar. When they moved, Grover could finally come to school all year round, so he decided he'd try out for the football team. The problem was that being from the hollers, Grover had pretty much never seen a football, much less a football game before. First time he dressed out for practice he didn't know where to put his cup. Neil told him it was a special noseguard only for running backs. Well, running back is exactly what Grover wanted to be, so he strung the daggone thing right over his nose and ran onto the field! Coach raised all kind of Cain with him and just about kicked him off the team right there. But then Coach changed his mind and gave him one more chance.

Good thing, too, because Grover turned out to be the best running back on the whole team—so good he's up for the Preston County Senior Trophy this year.

Everyone's finished dressing now, and it's almost time to head to the field. Grover's bouncing up and down like some kind of daggone jumping bean. Corduroy is cracking his knuckles. I'm still sitting down on this shiny metal bench, flexing my knee back and forth. I mutter a Hail Mary under my breath that the dang thing holds up for the entire game. It's got to.

Before we head out on the field, Coach calls us all around him. Like he's done before every game, he stretches out his hand and asks, "Who makes up this team, men?"

Corduroy puts his hand on top of Coach's and says, "Corduroy Mars!"

Grover is next. "Grover Jacobs!"

"Art Bishop!"

Every member of the team reaches out his hand and says his own name, as Coach looks him square in the eyes. I go last.

"Jimmy Cannon!"

Coach says his own name after mine. "Reginald Hainsworth!"

He looks at all of us. His face is serious. "I'm going to tell you something I've never said to any other team I've ever coached, boys." The room is silent.

"I've been around a heck of a long time. You know, I coached some of your daddies when they were coming up." He looks over at Art Bishop and Herbert Mathene.

"I gotta tell you, though, I've never coached a team like you in all my life." He pauses, looking each of us in the face, one by one, like he's taking snapshots with his eyes.

"A team isn't just a bunch of disjointed kids running off haphazard onto a ball field. You know that by now." His face is like a magnet, pulling us in.

"A team doesn't boil itself down to one person, either. Not on offense"—he looks over at Grover—"and not on defense"—he looks at me.

"Look at the man standing across from you," says Coach. We do. I find myself staring into Neil Fisher's eyes. For the first time in my life I notice they're green. It's uncomfortable, but neither of us is willing to look down.

"You're looking at the man who has it in his power to help you win the greatest game ever known to a Rowlesburg team," says Coach. "The one who's going to throw himself down for you today. The one who's going to be there pulling you up every time you fall."

Neil is staring at me hard. I'm staring right back at him.

"You're looking at nothing less than your own brother,

men. The one who's going to be there for you today and on every All Hallows' Eve for the rest of your life, when you and every person sitting out there in this stadium looks back and remembers today as the highest day in Rowlesburg football history.

"The man you're looking at is the buddy you'll tell your children about—and your children's children—how he helped you claw and scratch and beat the tar out of this Kingwood team today. He's the one you'll tell them stood by your side when *you*—you men standing here today, and no others that came before you or that will *ever* come after you—when *you* were on the team that won the first Rowlesburg championship."

We break the circle with a crack that echoes like a rifle shot. Our cheers drown out all hearing, and for a moment I am sight and nothing more. My eyes take in the fire thrown from my teammates' faces, branding each of them inside me forever. To the grave.

We blast out of the locker room into the bright lights of the stadium. The rush of night wind surges down my back as I run, sucking the cold air into my nose, breathing it out again, warmed. My knee feels pretty good. I only hope it stays that way.

The Rowlesburg crowd is tiny compared to the gargantuan number of Kingwood fans, but they fill the bleachers with their own brand of hometown warmth—

plaid flannel shirts and pint flasks. I scan the stands. Practically the whole town is here. Corduroy Mars's family is sitting all together—Stubby and the rest of his brothers, his cousins, second cousins, aunts and uncles—the whole lot. Rail is sitting next to them with Mr. Barton, the feed wholesaler, on his right, who I'll bet is the one that wagered him we're gonna lose today. And on his left is Thaddy Ore, whose eyes are fluttering up and down the field like little butterflies. His hands are clasped together beneath his chin, his bony knuckles propping up an overwhelmed, gleeful grin.

Way up top in the high seats are the other railroaders—Neil's daddy and his older brother, David, who's just back from the war, are sitting there, right next to Art Bishop's dad and Jerry Heath. Not too far from them sits my brother Mike, with his girlfriend, Viv. They're making eyes at each other, as usual these days. Bill's brought Audrey and their new baby, Patrick, who's half named after Dad. And next to them is Mom. She's chomping on her thumbnail, worried into a frenzy about my knee and Dad's wheezing, I'm sure. Beside her is an empty hole in the stands where Dad should be. I think of him sitting at home by himself on the porch—and on his birthday, too. Part of me feels sorry for him all sick and alone there, but the bigger part of me just wants to rub it in his face when we win. I ball up my fists. I hope he didn't have a big dinner tonight, because he's gonna be eating crow for dessert. And I'm gonna be the one that feeds it to him.

Coach's whistle echoes through the stadium. We run to him. This is it.

"We want first possession if we win the toss, boys," he says to Art and Grover. They nod, and run out onto the field for the coin toss. It hits me that, as senior captains, this is the last game they'll ever play for Rowlesburg. Their last chance for a championship. My stomach tightens in a knot of resolve.

Grover and Art are on the fifty-yard line shaking hands with that little Manny Pedersen and his co-captain. Manny was unstoppable in the backfield last year. But that was then. Most of his offensive line graduated last May, and this season it's been a whole new ball of wax, even if he *is* up for the Preston County Senior Trophy against Grover. And this year, I'm no freshman. As middle linebacker, Coach told me it's my personal job to shut him down. And that's exactly what I'm gonna do.

Grover pumps Manny's arm up and down hard, like they do in the hollers whenever they shake hands. Manny can't pull his own hand away fast enough. Grover just grins. He does it to the opposing team's co-captains every game. Thinks it throws them off balance.

The ref tosses the coin fifteen feet up into the air. It flips end over end as it goes up, reflecting the lights of the stadium like a series of flashbulbs. As it flickers its way back down, I know Art is calling heads. He always calls heads.

And it is! The referee pats Art on the shoulder. We've got the ball!

The muscles in my legs tighten as I run onto the field, fanning out with the rest of the team to receive the kick. Grover is already standing on our five-yard line, watching the Kingwood kicker line up. Our orange and black jerseys stand out like tiger skins against the grass, the perfect colors for a game on All Hallows' Eve.

The ref blows the whistle. The Kingwood kicker raises and lowers his hand, then stutter-steps towards the tee. The ball goes up high and straight. Grover races forward to catch it on the fifteen and is already in a flat-out run by the time he pulls it down. I shoot out in front of him, knocking a black and silver jersey left into one of his own teammates. It opens up a huge hole. Grover rushes past me into it. He's already to the thirty. The forty-five. *Holy mackerel*, he's over the fifty-yard line!

I chase behind him, but it's all Grover now. The Rowlesburg crowd roars as he jukes two of the Kingwood boys into tripping all over each other. He shoots up the sideline. It's unbelievable! There's only one Kingwood player left between him and the goal! Grover leans in and gives the guy a stiff-arm to the shoulder. They're a tangle of arms and legs tumbling down, but—*Holy Mother*

Mountain! Grover somehow stays on his feet! Touchdown, Rowlesburg River Lions!

Grover pumps his fist hard into the air as we race towards him like a swarm of orange and black screaming banshees. Art Bishop reaches him first and picks him clean up off his feet. The rest of us barrel down on them, banging Grover all over the helmet as Art lets him down and we line up for the extra point.

"It's good!" shouts the announcer over the PA system. "Seven-zero, Rowlesburg."

I slap Nobe Jenkins on the back as we run off the field. He's our field-goal kicker, our kickoff kicker, and our punter. When we get to the sideline, Coach motions Nobe over and talks to him in a low voice.

"Kick the ball away from number forty-four, Jenkins," Coach says. "That's the Pedersen boy. He's had a runback for a touchdown in every game Kingwood's won this season."

Nobe nods. "Got it, Coach."

"And Cannon." Coach looks over at me. "You know what to do whenever Pedersen *does* get the ball."

I nod and follow Nobe onto the field. I know what to do. Hit him so hard the spit flies clean out of his mouth.

Nobe is as good as his word and kicks a long one away from Pedersen. Their other receiver fields it, and Neil pastes him straightaway on his own fifteen-yard line.

I set up behind our linemen, stretching my knee out

behind me. So far, it's feeling pretty tolerable. Pretty soon Pedersen's gonna be thinking he has two shadows. Heck, he's gonna be *wishing* I was just a shadow by the end of the quarter!

The ball is snapped and I'm over the line before their offensive linemen can pull their knuckles up off the grass. I ignore a little twang in my knee and shoot between two of them into the backfield. It's a handoff to Pedersen, and I'm on him just as the ball is hitting his hands. I lower my shoulder and drive it into his belly. Hard.

He slams backwards onto the ground but manages to hang on to the ball. Pretty impressive, given how I laid him out. Most players would've coughed it up like a peppermint. Still, it's a good start. If we can hold them this set of downs, it'll definitely knock some of the wind out of their sails.

"A three-yard loss on the play," shouts the announcer. "Second and thirteen on the twelve-yard line."

The next play is another handoff to Pedersen. He shoots towards the middle, but I cut him down like a stalk of buckwheat for loss of another yard. He glares at me as he gets up and spits a wad into the grass. As I bend over to rub my knee, I lay one down in the turf, too, so he knows I mean business. I don't expect he's much used to getting stopped in the backfield. Well, I guess he'd better get himself used to it tonight.

The Rowlesburg fans are all riled up as our defense

spreads out over the field for third down. I look over into the stands and see Old Man Gatry standing up in the front row, leaning on his cane, yelling for all he's worth.

"Hold 'em, Rowlesburg!"

The Stags' quarterback hikes the ball and flicks a little screen to the right. Neil Fisher comes a-flying out of nowhere and intercepts the pass. There's nothing between him and the goal line. He speeds into the end zone without anyone on the Kingwood team so much as laying a hand on him. Touchdown!

The whole team piles on top of Neil. As we run off the field, we pass by Manny Pedersen on the sideline. He's scowling over at the Rowlesburg bleachers like he's gonna burn a hole right through them. I follow the direction of his stare and see old Mr. Gatry standing up again facing the crowd, shaking his cane over his head. He's leading another cheer.

"Rickety rickety rust," he shouts. "By God we'll win, we must!"

It catches on like brushfire through the stands, and by the time we take the field again, every Rowlesburg fan in the stadium is on his feet, chanting with Mr. Gatry and waving anything they can get their hands on that's orange and black. My heartbeat takes on the rhythm of the cheer and I completely forget about my knee. There's no way in the world we're gonna lose this game. The Kingwood players look like they can feel it, too. After we convert on the extra point, their black and silver jerseys are slow to jog back out onto the field. Some of the players are even walking. But not that Pedersen boy. He storms the field like he owns it and shouts at his teammates to do the same.

Jenkins kicks the ball high and long and away from Pedersen, just like he's supposed to. Their number sixty-five handles it and runs forward a yard. But then he laterals it back to Pedersen.

Me and Neil are down the field like a spray of buckshot, him to the right, me to the left. I charge through the Kingwood players like a Mallet engine until I'm right in front of Pedersen. He tries his little head fake on me, but I'm watching his belly button. Nobody can fake where their belly button's gonna go. I grab him around the chest and level him onto the ground at his own twenty-yard line.

"Daggumit!" he shouts, slamming his hand on the ground as I go to get up off him. In a rage, he jerks himself to his knees, knocking me sideways in the process. I hop to the right to catch my balance and suddenly feel a sharp *zing* in my knee. When I go to put my weight on it, it buckles straightaway underneath me. A smile curls around Pedersen's teeth as he watches me try to shake it off. A few seconds later I can put some pressure on it, but there's no hiding the fact that I'm limping as I head back to the line.

Coach notices, too. He's waving me off the field.

I hobble over to the sideline. Pedersen's watching me all the way.

"How bad is it there, Jimmy?" Coach asks.

"No big deal, Coach. Just a little sore."

Coach jacks up his eyebrows into a question mark. "Lemme see you bend it, son."

"What, you callin' me a liar?" I force a grin as I bend it. It hurts, but I'm not gonna let him know how much. "Honest, it's just fine, Coach."

Coach gives me the eye. I can tell he doesn't buy it. "Let's have you rest it for a few downs," he says.

"But Coach—"

He puts his hand up, then points to the bench. "Sit down, Jimmy. We need that knee to last the whole game."

I sit down and watch Boo Boo Avery run out onto the field in my place. Boo Boo's a nice enough guy, but he's about as slow as a Chevy up on blocks. Small, too. There's no way he's gonna stop a spiteful little back like Pedersen.

The next play Pedersen runs left past Boo Boo for twenty yards before Neil finally crosses the field to bring him down.

I stand up real quick and walk back over to Coach. I'm about ready to get down on my bad knee and beg him.

“Coach—” I start to say, but he cuts me off.

“I saw, Cannon. Now sit back down and rest.”

My knee’s still sore as I turn to head back to the bench, but I stop midstep as the Stags’ quarterback hikes the ball again. Pedersen runs left again past Boo Boo for another twenty yards.

“Cannon!” Coach turns and yells towards the bench. But I’m already there at his side. “Get back in there.”

I run onto the field, trying my best not to limp. As I pass the Stags’ huddle, Manny Pedersen sticks his head up and stares at my knee. It’s like he’s salivating, ready to hop on me like a flea on a dog.

We set for the next play and there’s not a doubt in my mind he’s heading right down my throat. He sets up in the backfield. We lock eyes. The ball is snapped and sure enough, he comes barreling straight at me. I brace my knee, clenching my teeth onto some deep-down grit I never knew I had, and slam him down hard pretty close to the line of scrimmage. Pedersen gets up slow.

I don’t.

When he finally gets to his feet, his jaw is clamped tight. His eyes slash at me like a couple of razors as he points his finger at my bad knee. I know it’s a threat, ’cause he’s sure as heck not asking me if it’s okay. I point my finger back at him. If that’s the way you wanna play, then you’re on, jerk. You’re not getting through me tonight, bad knee or no.

It's second and eight now. The Stags' quarterback fakes a pass, then laterals back to Pedersen. He sprints left towards the sideline, looking for room to cut downfield. I'm two steps behind, trying to close in on him. It's nothing but a footrace between the two of us now. If he turns the corner on me, he'll gain ten, maybe more. I can't let him.

I jack up the speed, forgetting the pain in my knee. Pedersen's rounding the corner as I launch myself into the air. My hands find his shoulder pads and grab for all they're worth. The rest of me keeps flying, knocking the both of us into the air and out of bounds for no gain on the play. I roll off him and straightaway take stock of my knee. It hurts, but nothing really seems the worse for wear.

Pedersen slams the ground with his hand again, then watches me close as I get to my feet. I do my durndest not to limp as I run back to the huddle, but it's getting harder to hide the pain.

It's third down now, and we've gotta hold 'em here. Pedersen goes out for a pass, but I'm covering him closer than his next of kin. The quarterback hesitates. There's nowhere to throw. He looks downfield, but it's too late. Neil blazes through the right side of their line heading straight for his blind side. Plow! The guy slams to the ground like he's been run over by a train.

Neil is up in half a second, stabbing his fist into the

air. I limp on over to him and grab him by the jersey, getting right up in his face. "We're gonna be the daggone Preston County champions tonight, Neil!" I shout.

We turn to line up again and realize that the Kingwood quarterback is still down, curled up into a ball on the ground, clutching at his ribs. The Kingwood coach is running over to him with a few other men from the Stags' sideline. In a minute, a stretcher is carried onto the field.

As they're lifting the guy onto it, Neil nudges me in the side. "Look there, Jimmy."

He points past the stretcher, over at Pedersen, who's standing on the line of scrimmage. He's scowling as he drives his fist hard into his hand. But it's not just anger I read in his eyes. It's rage. The rage that comes when you know your team's gonna lose but you just can't admit it.

Suddenly, Pedersen looks up and sees us staring at him. He gets a look on his face the likes of which I've never seen before on a ballplayer. His lips draw back, baring his teeth. His eyes are wide open like a chained dog's. A dog that hasn't been fed in a week. A dog that wants to take a huge hunk out of my neck. Or my knee.

Neil and I turn our eyes away from him to look at each other.

"Whoa," I say.

"Whoa is right," says Neil. "Looks like he's losing

more than the game." He tries to snarl back his mouth like Pedersen, and we both laugh.

There's thirty-five seconds left on the clock before the end of the first quarter. Coach waves us in to the sideline as the medics work to carry the Kingwood quarterback off the field. I limp over as he gathers us around him. My knee's really talking to me now. But I'm not listening to it. Coach is talking.

"Okay, men, this is it," he barks. "They're going for a first down and their second-string quarterback's coming in, which means they'll be running the ball. You men in the secondary hang close to the line and don't worry about a pass." He looks over at me. "Jimmy—how's that knee?"

"A-okay, Coach," I say. I'm only lying a little.

Coach eyes me but lets it pass. "Okay, boys," he says. His voice is intense, like there's a volcano in his mouth and he's trying to keep it from blowing too soon. "Don't let up now, even for a second. This is your game. This is your championship. No one can take it away from you, unless you let them. You understand me?"

"Yeah!!" we scream back at him. We sure as heck do understand.

"Now get out there and win this ball game!"

I storm the field with my team and set up behind our linemen. The Kingwood players are set, too, but there's no spark in their faces. Their eyes are cast down on the grass between us, refusing to meet my stare. All except for Pedersen. I see him in the backfield with that same crazed expression on his face. And he's looking right at me.

I listen for the snap, and spring forward as soon as the ball moves. The ball's to Pedersen and I'm slipping through his tired line like summer butter. There's no one between the two of us now. Pedersen sees me and takes a few rushed steps backwards, trying to get more room to run, but I'm on him like his own sweat. He tries to juke, but I'm already there, pounding him facedown into the turf for loss of another five yards.

As I roll off him and start to get up, I feel a yank at my knee. A hurricane of pain rips through my leg as it's suddenly wrenched out from under me. My teeth clank together as my jaw hits the ground, leaving a piece of chipped tooth floating around in my spit. I'm on my stomach, the wind knocked out of me. And someone's sitting on my back, twisting my bad knee in a vise grip. I don't have to look back to know it's Pedersen.

The jolt to my jaw has my eyes rolling back in my head. Dark is gathering from the outer edges, moving in fast. I hear yelling. I can vaguely make out the black and white stripes of the refs moving towards me. My knee wrenches again as they try to pull Pedersen off me, but he won't let go. Pain rips through my leg. I feel myself losing consciousness. I spit out my broken tooth to keep myself from choking.

Somewhere in the back of my head I hear Neil Fisher's voice. His yelling pierces the blackness, through my closed eyes. Without warning I'm knocked from my stomach onto my side—Pedersen's weight is off me, but the wrenching doesn't stop. My eyes flutter open, my sight blurred by the pain. I feel an elbow poking in my side; the black and white stripes of the referees' shirts are backing away. Where the heck are they going?

I close my eyes, trying to squint back the pain. There's the sound of hard slapping. *Whack.* I feel myself passing out. *Whack.* But the grip on my leg is finally relaxing, letting go. *Whack-whack.* Suddenly, my knee pops back into place. A wave of nausea surges. Then there is nothing.

Next thing I realize, my whole body is bobbing up and down. When I open my eyes, the stands are rushing by, angry Kingwood faces smearing together as I'm carried off the field. But I'm not on a stretcher. Neil and Grover are carrying me. Grover's got me under the arms. Neil's got me by the legs, careful not to grip too near my knee.

I crane my neck, trying to understand what's happening. My whole team is around me in a circle, like Secret Service men around President Truman. The refs are there with them, too, along with both teams' coaches. Their arms are up, trying to make a way for us through the irate crowd. I look up at Neil's face. It's white. His eyes are scanning the throngs of screaming Kingwood fans.

One of the refs is shouting at the crowd.

"Out of the way, we gotta get the boy to the hospital!"

The hospital? I don't need a hospital. I look down at my knee. It aches like the devil, but it doesn't seem broken or anything. If I could put my weight down on it I could tell for sure. I wiggle my legs, wanting to get down.

"I don't need a—" But Neil grips me tighter, cutting me off.

"Shut up, Jimmy," he says like a ventriloquist, hardly moving his mouth. "Pretend you do. The Kingwood crowd's getting ready to lynch us."

I look past Neil's head out to the crowd again. The Kingwood fans have poured down out of the stands and onto the field, pressing in on us from all sides. Some of the drunk ones are yelling at the refs, refusing to move out of the way. Trickles of Rowlesburg fans are seeping through the huge Kingwood crowd, trying to make a sort of buffer around our whole team. I can see why Neil looks scared. These Kingwood fans ain't just a regular crowd anymore. They're a mob.

"Why? What the heck happened?" I ask, trying to call up the last minute of the game in my sore head. Neil almost cracks a smile, then tells me to shut up again.

But Grover bends his head down to my ear. "The refs couldn't get Pedersen to let go of your knee."

I remember that much.

"So Neil jumped him," whispers Grover. "Beat the living snot outta the boy 'til he let go of you. Knocked him clean out."

I look at Neil. He's got a little grin on his face, even as he keeps scanning the sea of angry faces. It's not me the Kingwood fans want to get at. It's Neil.

Suddenly, I realize we've stopped moving forward. Shouts are raging back and forth between the Kingwood and Rowlesburg fans. Neil is biting his lower lip. It's like I'm sitting on top of a keg of gunpowder, with people waving lit matches on every side. Somebody better do something. And soon.

What the heck, it might as well be me.

I close my eyes and groan as loud as I can. "Aarrghhhhh . . ."

The shouts begin to quiet down.

I groan out again, even louder, ending in the most pathetic whimper I can muster.

"For God's sake," shouts one of the refs. "Let the boy through. Settle your scores later."

The crowd stays quiet; I hold my breath, then groan again. Slowly, the rustle of winter coats begins to brush past my ears. We're moving forward.

I keep moaning and whimpering a little here and there, and in another minute, we're in the locker room, safe behind barred doors. Neil and Grover lay me on one of the benches, my eyes still closed. I hear Coach's voice.

"For Pete's sake, don't put him down, boys. Get him out to the car so we can get him to the hospital."

I open my eyes and give one more fake groan. Neil and Grover bust out laughing. The rest of the team does, too, as I stand up to try out my knee. It's sore as heck, but it still works. I can put a good chunk of my weight on it. In a couple of weeks it'll be good as new.

Before Coach can say a word, there's a hard knock on the door. He furrows his eyebrows at us to be quiet, unbars the door and steps out. There's a murmur of voices in the hallway, and in a minute he's back with a vacant sort of look on his face. We all stare at him.

"The referees called a forfeit, boys," he says quietly. "Well—"

But Neil cuts him short by slamming his fist on the bench with a force that jolts us all. He looks at us fiercely, then drops his eyes, shaking his head back and forth. The whole room deflates like a ruptured tire.

"If I'd-a kept my head . . . ," Neil says, still looking down at the floor. We can practically see the rest of the sentence noodling through his mind. It's noodling through all ours, too. If he'd-a kept his head, we'd be Preston County champions right now.

We were so close. So daggone close.

Suddenly, Grover slams his hand down on the bench next to Neil. Neil jerks his head up. The rest of us do, too.

"If you'd-a kept your head, Neil," Grover says, "Jimmy's knee'd be torn off at the bone right now, ain't that right, Jimmy?" He looks defiantly at Coach, then at me.

"I expect so," I say, nodding my head. It sure felt like it was heading that way.

Grover stands up on the bench and looks down at us. "What the heck do refs know about champions, anyhow?" he yells. "If standing up for your buddy is reason to forfeit, then the championship ain't worth a piece of dung anyway!" He looks down at Neil. "I wish I'd-a had the gumption to jump Pedersen right along with you!"

Grover hops off the bench onto Neil and me both, and the rest of the team piles on top of us chanting, "*Fi-sher, Fi-sher, Fi-sher, Fi-sher . . .*"

After a minute or two Coach gets up onto the bench, waving his arms for us to quiet down. "Hang on a second, boys," he chuckles. "I need to tell you something."

He looks at us all and lets out a laugh. "I probably *don't* have to tell you I've never seen a game like this before in all my life. You boys played your hearts out, and I know if we'd gone the full four quarters, we'd have beat the tar out of them."

He looks over at Neil. "And even though it's never been part of my playbook to coldcock the opposing team's star player, I'll bet Jimmy here is mighty grateful that you did, Neil."

I nod and slap Neil on the back.

"And," Coach goes on, "I happen to know a couple of other people who are grateful for it, too."

Neil looks up at him. "Who?" he asks.

"The referees."

"The *refs*?" says Neil.

"Yeah, the refs," says Coach. "It would have made a heck of a lawsuit against them if another player had broken Jimmy's leg like that under their watch."

Neil frowns. "Then what the heck are they doing making us forfeit?" he growls.

"Well, that leads me to the thing I need to tell you," says Coach.

We all stare at him.

"You boys misunderstood when I came back in here announcing the forfeit."

There is complete silence.

"The refs called a forfeit by *Kingwood,*" he says. "You—the Rowlesburg River Lions—are the 1946 Preston County champions! Congratulations, men!"

After the celebrating; after waiting for the diehards in the mob to leave; after I finally talk Coach into not taking me to the hospital, we're back at Rowlesburg High School. It's after nine-thirty when Coach congratulates us all one last time and pulls off in his Chevy.

I start talking about where we'll go to continue the celebration, hoping to avoid what I know is coming next. But Neil says what everyone else is thinking.

"Let's go pay a visit to your dad, Jimmy."

I clear my throat, trying to come up with any reason not to. I don't need another earful of his bull. Not after having to be carried off the field. Not after only winning by a daggone forfeit.

"Dad's probably asleep by now," I tell them. "You don't want to go waking up a sick old man."

Neil looks at me like I've sprouted three extra heads. "There's no way on God's green earth he's gonna be asleep after this game," he says.

The rest of the team lets out shouts of agreement, and they begin moving in a bunch towards my house, jockeying for position to be in the front. I hobble fast around them and put up my hands as a train whistle bellows out of the darkness behind me.

"Look, don't you already know what he's gonna say?" I look at their stupid smiles and clench my fists. "He's just gonna tell us we didn't win every single game. That we're only the Preston County champions because it was forfeited to us, not because we won it ourselves. Don't you see?"

Neil walks up to me and puts his hand on my shoulder.

"'Course your dad's gonna say that, Jimmy. But we *are* the Preston County champions, right, men?! We won that game fair and square. Hard-fought, too. 'Specially by you. He's gotta admit that much."

He drops his hand from my shoulder to lead a River Lion cheer. My arms droop by my sides as the rest of the team starts walking again. They just don't get it. Dad never admits that he's wrong.

I stand still for a minute, then follow along behind them, rounding the corner of Rail's store, walking the tracks until we get within sight of our porch. I see Mom hovering worriedly over Dad as he sits there in his rocking chair, asleep with Amos on his lap. When she sees us coming towards them, she runs lickety-split inside the house. Guess she doesn't want to hear any of what Dad's gonna say, either.

The team is quiet as I hobble my way up behind them to the porch.

"See?" I whisper. "He's asleep. Now let's go."

I no sooner shut my mouth than my father's eyes pop wide open.

"Well, well, well," he snorts. "What do we have here?"

"Just the 1946 Preston County football champions, Mr. Cannon," says Neil.

"So you won the game, boys?"

There's an uncomfortable silence. Technically a forfeit is counted as a win. But we didn't actually win-win. And he knows it, too. I know darn well that the first thing Rail did after the game was come right over and give Dad the play-by-play, including how it ended. Dad's just toying with us, trying to get us to admit a forfeit isn't the same as a win. Trying to make us believe we're not really undefeated. Trying to twist it all up into making himself be right somehow.

Well, he's not.

"Yeah, Dad, we won," I say, looking straight into his eyes.

He looks past the other players at me, chewing the inside of his lip, like he's trying to decide what to say. My eyes stay focused right in on his, and tonight, for the first time in my whole entire life, I feel like I can see right through him. Like a ghost. He finally snorts and looks away, then lets out a chuckle.

"Well, boys," he says, "I guess you owe me a debt of gratitude, then."

I bite my tongue, but Neil laughs out loud and twists his finger inside his ear, like it's all plugged up. "Sorry, Mr. Cannon, I must've misheard you. What'd you say again?"

"I said, Neil," says Dad, raising his voice so as not to be misheard again, "I guess you boys owe me a debt of gratitude."

This time I can't hold myself back. "A debt of gratitude? For what? For not believing we could win? For telling us every week we were gonna lose? Yeah, thanks a lot, Dad."

I roll my eyes and turn to go. It doesn't faze Dad at all. He chuckles again and calls after me. "Ah, Jimmy, but there's where you're wrong. Why, I knew you boys could win the championship from the very first scrimmage," he says. "You just needed someone to tell you that you couldn't."

I cut my eyes back towards him and see just about the orneriest grin I've ever seen on a person. And even though I don't really want to, I can't help but crack a half smile myself. Because I know I'll never understand that man. Even if I live to see another hundred All Hallows' Eves.

A DAY AT THE M&K

ALL HALLOWS' EVE 1947

A steam engine is blowing outside my bedroom window, and my father's just getting up, which means it's four o'clock in the morning. I'm never awake this early, but for some reason today I just can't get back to sleep. Downstairs the kitchen light *cha-chinks* as Dad pulls its metal chain. I slide my feet out from under my quilt and sit up on the edge of the bed. It crosses my mind to bury my head back underneath the pillow, but I just can't shake this feeling in my gut—the feeling that Something's gonna happen. After all, it's All Hallows' Eve. And Dad's turning double sixes today.

I get dressed as fast as I can, tiptoe down the stairs and creep up on Dad as he sits by his oatmeal bowl in the kitchen. His eyes are closed and he's bent over the dinette table fingering his painted rosary beads, worn all the way through to the warm hickory wood. I hug the door frame, standing perfectly still so he won't notice me. He rolls the beads between his thumb and his forefinger, one by one by one. His lips are moving, but no sound comes out.

My father isn't like most of my friends' fathers. He's more like their grandfathers, or even their great-grandfathers. Old as he is, though, he's still built just like a fireplug. Heck, any stranger could tell just by looking at him that he's not someone to mess with. Just ask any one of us boys. Avoiding his wrath has been a part-time job for all three of us.

But this morning he looks smaller and thinner than usual, with his dark pants hanging loose around his legs like the wattle of an old turkey flopping loose around its neck. He seems to have been feeling lots better lately, but the pneumonia he had again this past summer really took its toll on his body. How could I not have noticed until today?

I'm sure he doesn't know I'm standing here. He would never let me watch him for so long if he knew. The train whistle blows again.

He snorts that snort of his.

"What you doing up so early, Jimmy?" His eyes aren't even open.

I don't know what to say. I can't tell him I'm waiting

for Something to happen. And I *sure* as heck can't tell him I'm watching him look old.

He opens his eyes and stands up, putting his rosary beads into his pants pocket and his oatmeal bowl into the sink.

"Off to work."

I look down at the floor, not really knowing what to say, and am surprised to realize that I don't want him to go. He puts on his felt hat and makes his way to the screen door. As he opens it, I look up and try to make conversation to the back of his head.

"Happy birthday, Dad."

He turns around and looks at me. The deep creases around his eyes soften for a moment. He snorts again.

During the past few months I've been doing a lot of listening to my father's snorts, partly because he seems to be snorting more, but mostly because I've been trying to figure out what his snorts really mean. So far I've figured out that the reason he's snorting more is because his emphysema is getting worse. Talking takes more air for his lungs than a snort does.

Understanding what his snorts mean has been a harder question to figure. When I was younger, I always thought he snorted at me because I was bugging him. But lately I've realized that he doesn't just snort when he's bothered. Heck, he snorts all the time. He snorted at me last year when I finally got up the courage to tell him how bad I wanted to quit school and go to work on the railroad. I thought he was liable to kill me after that snort. But then the next semester when I showed him a report card full of A's and B's—even in Mr. Kaylor's chemistry class—he snorted the exact same way.

Then I realized that he snorts after jokes and stories, too. He snorts instead of saying "yes," and he snorts instead of saying "no." Heck, he even snorted when Bill told him he was going to be a granddad again this year. Then out of nowhere Dad slapped Bill on the back so hard it sent them both to spluttering.

It was when he snorted at the news that Mike and Viv were getting married that I finally figured out you couldn't tell *what* the heck my father was feeling from his snort. It just tells you that he's feeling *something.* I figure it's kind of like the whistle on an old Mallet engine: if you hear it, you know a train is coming. Or maybe it's more like a sacrament—an outward and visible sign that points to an inward and spiritual something or another. But if you want to know what that something or another actually *is,* you have to keep a lookout and find it somewhere else.

I'm looking to find it right now. I see this white-headed old man with a sort of smile crinkled up in a wad around his eyes. It's not around his mouth. You have to look in his eyes.

"Come on," he says through the crinkles. Then out of

nowhere he says the words I've been waiting to hear since I was a little kid: "You come to work with me today, Jimmy. It's about time you learned a real thing or two about the Baltimore & Ohio Railroad."

I let out a smile big enough to split my face in two. I've snuck around the M&K Junction my whole life, but Dad has never once officially taken me to work with him.

This is the Something I've been waiting for!

He lets out another snort and turns to walk through the screen door. I follow on his heels, almost tripping over Amos. We walk in a line down the steps of the porch—my father, Amos, then me—and head across the grass to Main Street. Amos has never really liked me—heck, he's never really liked anybody excepting my father. He keeps turning around and meowing as if to tell me I should go back home and leave the two of them alone.

I guess he has good reason. Ever since he was a scrawny little inkspot of a kitten, he's walked my father to work as far as the old train trestle. He's as big and mean as an old badger now, but the ritual's still the same. Even though I'm almost never up by the time they leave the house, I sure as heck know how it ends every morning. About twenty minutes after they leave, they come back home, and my father yells at my mother through the screen door, loud enough for the whole neighborhood to hear, "Mary Etta, can't you keep this dagburn cat away from me?"

It's like an alarm clock. And you know, that cat never follows him a second time in the morning.

I don't even think about trying to displace Amos from his rightful place beside my father. I drop a few steps behind them, picking up their leisurely pace. They look less like a couple of beat-up old cronies than an older couple in love, sauntering slowly down the street. Every now and again Amos'll rub his head up against my father's brown pant legs. And Dad'll snort and snatch at his tail.

When we get to the train trestle, Dad turns around quickly to take Amos home again. They almost bump right into me.

"Dagburn cat," my father mutters. He's forgotten I'm with them.

As we turn back towards the house, I start thinking how sort of stupid it is for Dad to always talk that way about Amos when I know durn well how much he loves that cat. I've got half a mind to tell him so, but I decide at the last minute just to bite my tongue instead. I don't want him to change his mind about taking me to work.

The three of us get back to the house. Mom is already up and cooking in the kitchen. My father yells the usual about Amos through the screen door. "Mary Etta, can't you keep this dagburn cat away from me?"

But Mom ignores him, talking to me instead. "What are you doing up so early, Jimmy?"

"He's coming to work with me, Mary Etta," Dad says.

She opens the screen door and frowns. "The boy can't go to work with you, William Patrick. He has to go to school today."

"He doesn't have to go to school today if I say he doesn't."

She slams the door closed, which is her way of giving in. If she'd really put her foot down, I wouldn't be going anywhere at all today, and Dad and I both would be getting an earful to boot.

My father snorts and looks at me, shrugging his shoulders and turning to begin his walk to work again. Amos doesn't follow him this time, but I do. Again down Main Street, again up the steep path to the tracks at the train trestle. The trestle is really a long steel bridge stretching across the Cheat River, wide enough for two engines going in opposite directions to pass. I hesitate, looking both ways before venturing onto the footpath that runs between the two tracks. My father just glances at his pocket watch and strides out onto the bridge.

"Train won't be here for another twenty minutes, Jimmy," he says without looking back.

I trust his watch—he has it calibrated once a week at Watson's Store like every other railroader in town does—but I look both ways again, just to make sure. A few summers ago I got caught on the bridge when a train was coming. Wound up jumping, fishing pole and all, into the swimming hole twenty feet below. I know—at least in theory—it's perfectly safe to stay on the far side of the path while a train rushes by. But there's something unsettling about a steam engine when it's charging at you like that. You can get so caught up in watching it churn that you completely forget to move yourself out of its way. And there's no way of stopping one when it's coming right at you, that's for sure. Living in a railroad town all my life I've known too many people who've gotten themselves run over. I guess that's probably one of the reasons I've always wanted to be a machinist instead of an engineer. Machinists fix what's wrong with the engines. They don't have to try and stop them.

I take a breath and run onto the path. My father's never wrong—about trains, I mean. When we get across the bridge, the M&K Junction will almost be in sight. That's where we're headed. It's where Dad's worked pretty much every day of his life since practically the turn of the century. Heck, between him and his daddy and granddaddy, my family's either laid or worked every inch of this track running on both sides of the M&K—east, coming down the Cranberry Grade to Rowlesburg, and west coming all the way over from Grafton.

"Will Bill and Mike be there this morning?" I ask, finally catching up to him.

"Mike will. And Bill's coming in on the next train.

He's subbing as fireman on the 7049 out of Tunnelton this morning."

My brother Bill's worked for the railroad since he dropped out of school in '38. Dad didn't want him to, even way back then. Heck, ever since I was a little kid Dad's been telling us the railroad's no place to build a life anymore. Said it was going to change for the worse. New-fangled trains were going to come, he said, that would take fewer men to maintain. Different kind of engine. Different kind of fuel. Diesel. He said they'd put three-fourths of the town out of work.

But the diesels never came—around these parts at least—so we boys always figured Dad didn't really know what he was talking about. Bill didn't listen to him, at any rate. Neither did Mike. And I don't plan to, either. The railroad's in the Cannon blood. And I figure there'll always be a place to work in Rowlesburg for a man who can fix a steam engine. Even though lately I've started to hear other railroaders talking a lot more about the diesels, too.

I jump off the end of the bridge, glad to be off it. As we follow the tracks around the bend, the M&K Junction is coming up just beyond that last clump of locust trees. The junction is where the brick shop is—where all the exciting work gets done on the trains.

As we walk on, the hissing of the river is overcome by the clunk and clatter of metal pounding metal. You can always hear the M&K before you can see it. The pounding makes my pulse race. Even Dad's pace picks up as we pass the last few trees. He can't help it. When the railroad's in your blood, it draws you like a pump draws water from the ground.

When we clear the trees, we see a big Mallet engine sitting over the pits, like an old army sergeant ready to bark orders at the enlisted men.

"Air brakes almost went out on that Mallet yesterday coming down the Cranberry Grade back from Terra Alta," Dad says. "There ain't but a handful of men who could stop a moving train on that hill with hardly no brakes at all. Thank God Bishop was brakeman."

As we near the shop, the clanking gets louder and the track splinters off into four parallel branches. Two sets of rails run right into the brick shop, and the other two run over the outdoor pits where the Mallet is sitting. We walk by the interlocking tower, where Bob Deane and a group of other men are lighting up their morning smokes. Little Thaddy Ore is pushing a long-handled broom behind them, cleaning up their cigarette butts and the cinders that have blown from the overnight trains. He catches sight of me and Dad, and his eyes blink quickly to the ground, then skip shyly back up towards us. Two of his fingers uncurl from around the broom handle and bend in the smallest of waves.

My father snorts. "Morning, boys."

The rest of the men straighten themselves up. "Good morning, Mr. Cannon." Bob Deane nods at me. He was in Bill's class in school. "Is that a new machinist you got with you there, Mr. Cannon?"

My father snorts again. "I durn well sure hope not, Bob."

Bob laughs. "If he's anything like his older brothers, he'll be second in charge here by the end of the day."

My father chuckles, but shoots him a look that says that's enough. Bob winks at me and goes back to his smoke.

We're heading towards the Mallet now. She's a gleaming beauty, no more than a couple years old. I'd give my eyeteeth for a chance to get under her. If I'm lucky, I'll find a way to today when Dad's not looking. Maybe when Bill gets in.

Bill usually doesn't work as a fireman on the engines. Firemen just keep the fire going in the firebox and help make sure there's the right amount of water in the boiler to make enough steam to get over the mountains—without running dry and blowing to high heaven. Actually, it takes a lot of skill to be a good fireman. Bill can do it—heck, Bill can do pretty much any job on a train—but he thinks it's kind of boring. He's really a machinist. He gets to crawl down underneath the engines in the pits and make sure they're working right from the ground up. Just like I'm gonna do.

Just as I think I recognize Sonny McCormick's knees propped up on a sawhorse under the Mallet, I feel a punch to the back of my shoulder.

"What are you doing here, Jimmy? You ought to be in school." It's my brother Mike. He falls into step beside us.

"You sound just like Mary Etta," I tell him. He screws his face up into a pretzel. He can't stand being compared to Mom.

"He's come with me today so he can see why he's never gonna work on the railroad," Dad says. His voice is pointed.

I roll my eyes.

But Mike furrows his eyebrows. "As if you can keep a Cannon off the tracks," he mutters.

Dad snorts. "Come with me, the both of you." He says it almost like we're in some kind of trouble. Mike and I drop in step behind him as Mike flips me a couple of times on the back of the head with his knuckle. I turn around and jab at him until he stops.

We follow Dad into his office at the shop. It's a large room at the end of the building, with exposed brick-and-mortar walls and one large bright window that faces out onto the main tracks. The sharp sounds of metal being cut buzz into the room from the main hull of the shop as Dad sits down behind his huge oak desk. Mike and I have stopped swatting at each other and stand still in front of him, dwarfed. If the Mallet engine is an army sergeant,

Dad's definitely the general. His face is different now than it was sitting at home in front of his cereal bowl. His jaw is set hard as he scans the train log that sits in the center of his desk. There is no smile crinkled up behind his eyes here. He takes a pack of cigarettes out of his suit coat pocket, curls up his lip and pulls one out with his teeth. For a moment he looks just like a snarling dog.

I look over at Mike, who raises his eyebrows impatiently at me. I raise my eyebrows back. There's no rushing Dad when he's doing something. At best, you get a snort. We might as well just stay quiet and wait.

My eyes scan the room. Other than the desk and a file cabinet, it's pretty bare. There's a door to the left that leads into the main work area of the shop. The smell of oil seeps through it into the office. It's the same smell that hangs on my father every night when he comes home. I close my eyes and breathe it in.

"Okay, boys," says Dad, finally looking up. "You're going to be the first to see the plans." There's some kind of mischief lurking behind his eyes now.

Mike and I look at each other. "The plans?" says Mike. "What plans?"

Dad snorts. "The plans for the new addition to the shop." He bends over his desk and unrolls a blueprint, turning it to face us.

Mike's eyes light up. "You're expanding the shop?" he says, pouring himself over the blueprint. "That's great!"

"Yup," says Dad. "For the diesels."

An engine lets out a big huff of steam right outside the window. Mike's face falls. He looks across at Dad. "The diesels?" he says. "You've got to be kidding."

Dad's eyes narrow. "We're scheduled to start servicing them here beginning this May." He leans across the desk. "Steam engines are on their way out, Mike. Whether you like it or not."

It's Mike's turn to narrow his eyes. He leans in towards Dad, bracing both hands on top of the desk. "You've been saying the diesels are coming for the last ten years. What the hell makes you think it's really gonna happen now?"

My eyes go wide. I can't believe Mike cussed at Dad. We boys can cuss *around* him all we want, so long as Mom isn't around, but no matter how wrong he's ever been, I've never even thought about cussing *at* him.

Dad stands up straight as a rail. "Word's come down from Baltimore. And if you want to keep your job at this dagburn railroad, you'll sure as Hades learn about the diesels. That's *if* you even get to keep your job. The furloughs are coming, Mike. And you're practically last man hired. I never met such a dagburn dumb kid in all my life. You'll be out on your ear within the span of a year if you don't figure this thing out."

Mike's lips are drawn up like a cinch sack, his hands balled into fists pressing down hard on top of the blueprints. For a second I think he's going to go after Dad, right across the desk. He glares into Dad's eyes for several seconds, then jerks himself upright, knocking the blueprints to the floor. He storms out of the room without picking them up.

Dad snatches up the blueprints and shoves them back onto the desk. His jaw is rigid as he drums his fingers furiously over them. I wanna leave. Right now. Out the door, right behind Mike. Pretend I never saw any durn blueprints. Go bury myself under that Mallet engine.

But I can't.

Slowly, Dad's hands transition from ferocious drumming to methodically smoothing the wrinkles out of the plans. Over and over, he rubs the blueprints with open palms, back and forth. Back and forth. With each stroke of the paper his body deflates a little.

Finally, he speaks, still looking down at the desk. "A hundred and fifty men work on this railroad, and a hundred of them are going to lose their jobs within the next nine months." He looks up at me with his deep granite eyes. "And most of the lucky fifty are going to be transferred to Cumberland." He takes in a breath and wheezes out a long sigh as he rolls up the plans into a tight tube. "Change comes, Jimmy. It'll thunder down the tracks towards you like an engine with the brakes gone out. And sometimes, there ain't a dagburn thing you can do to stop it."

He pauses, looking every last one of his sixty-six years. And then some.

"This is going to hit Rowlesburg hard, son. A man's gotta learn how to read the times or else be crushed by them. For Pete's sake, you could do anything with your life besides work on the railroad. You could go into the service, or find work in Washington. Why, with your grades you could even go on to college, Jimmy."

He turns his eyes away from me towards the window that looks out onto the tracks.

"Promise me, Jimmy . . . promise me you'll—"

His words are eclipsed by an explosion outside that rings like a rifle shot through the mountains. He jumps to his feet and bolts out the door. I follow him.

"What the heck was that?" someone yells.

Men are flooding out of the shop with question marks wrinkled deep into their foreheads. Mike is with them. They pool like an eddy in a circle around my father, looking for an explanation on his face. It's not there. At least not as far as I can see. What I do see is serious. Worry. Or is it—fear?

Bob Deane breaks into the center of the circle. "The explosion came from up the Cheat River Grade, sir."

Dad looks at his watch. "Is the 7049 out of Tunnelton in yet?"

Several men shake their heads.

"It's three minutes late, sir," says Bob.

Dad snorts. "Oh my God," he says. His face has become as white as his hair.

"Holy mother," whispers Bob. He looks down at me. He can't meet my eyes but for a second before looking down at the ground.

Panic whips through me. "What, Bob?" I ask, frantically scanning the faces in the circle of men. My eyes land on Mike. "What the heck's going on?" I ask him.

But like the others, Mike just keeps looking at Dad.

I turn and look at him, too.

"Dad?" I ask.

My father looks at me, then looks away. His mouth twists and he takes in a deep chestful of air, like he's getting ready to say something. But Bob interrupts him before he can.

"Maybe it wasn't the engine, sir. Maybe . . . maybe it was an explosion over at the cement plant."

We hear the pounding of feet. A second later the circle of men opens and Jerry Heath runs into the middle of it. He stops in front of my father, panting hard.

"Buddy Boyer stopped me on the bridge, Mr. Cannon," Jerry says between breaths. "Said he was driving . . . down the Manheim Road . . . and when he looked across the river . . . Engine suddenly blew . . ."

He puts his head down between his knees to catch his wind.

Dad draws in a sharp breath and wheezes suddenly. "Bill . . ."

Before I can even think straight, Neil Fisher's dad steps into the center of the circle with me and my father.

"My boy David was engineer on that train this morning, W. P." He looks into my father's eyes, searching for an answer. My father just wheezes and stares grimly back at him.

Jerry finally catches his breath, oblivious to the conversation. "Said the boiler must've blown forty feet into the air."

Gasps go around the circle like we've all been sucker punched. Everyone knows when an engine blows like that, the fireman and the engineer never survive.

Dad takes a quick step back from Mr. Fisher, suddenly unsteady on his feet. "Dear God in heaven," he whispers.

I run over and steady him by the elbow.

"Dad?" I'm not sure whether I'm asking if he's okay or if Bill is really dead.

He doesn't answer.

"Dad?" I say again.

But my father stands still, frozen in front of me, wrapped with Mr. Fisher in a stare that separates them from all the rest of us. Even though I've got him gripped tight around the elbow, it's like he doesn't feel my touch at all. His other hand flies to his chest, gripping at the shirt buttons just over his heart.

I hear a sudden shout from outside the circle, but my eyes stay fixed on Dad. And his eyes stay locked with Mr. Fisher's. More voices join the shouting now, and I feel the weight of the other men's stare in my direction. But when I look up at them, they're not looking at me. They're looking behind me, their eyes wide as if they'd seen a ghost. I turn, my eyes following their stare.

Like a curtain being drawn back, several of the men step aside.

And there in front of me is my brother Bill. Little Thaddy Ore is standing beside him, pulling him by the hand towards the center of the circle.

"H-h-he's been in the john all morning, Mr. Cannon," stutters Thaddy. A few of the men beside him let themselves smile.

My father wheezes again and breaks his stare with Mr. Fisher to look on Bill. His eyes are wet, his chin trembling.

"Bill?" he says. His voice is as gravelly as the ground beneath us. "You . . . was supposed to be on that train."

There is complete silence. We all stare at Bill.

"I switched off, sorta sick to my stomach at the last minute," he says.

I take a deep breath at the sound of his voice. He's real.

Mr. Fisher's still staring at my father. "Did my boy David switch, too?" he asks, not moving his eyes.

Bill lowers his head. "No, Mr. Fisher."

My brother Bill might be alive again, but Mr. Fisher's boy is still dead.

And there's another man dead in place of Bill.

"Who'd you switch with, son?" Dad asks.

Bill's face goes pale as we wait for him to speak the dead man's name. Every face in the circle is pinched. Every heart beating for its brother.

"Willie Garrison," he whispers.

The circle exhales a groan, and in the back a cry goes up.

It's Benji Garrison, Willie's younger brother. He's only a couple years older than I am. Benji busts forward into the center of the circle, stopping barely a foot in front of me. I start to back away from him, but his eyes grip me tight and won't let go.

His stare splits me in two.

His brother. My brother. Suddenly dead. Suddenly not dead.

I rip my eyes away and look over at the tracks—at my father, at Bill, at the town just beyond the river. I wanna run. Away from them all.

Towards them all.

But the only durn thing I can do is just stand here. Stand here and wait for whatever comes next.

THE MIDNIGHT TRAIN

ALL HALLOWS' EVE 1948

There's only one key to Rail's store, and Rail keeps it in his front left pants pocket, right next to his snot rag. No one's allowed to touch it—the key, I mean—excepting for himself. Not that anyone'd want to, given where he keeps it. Still, snot rag or not, a key would be nice to have on nights like tonight, when it's long past closing time and Rail's still nowhere to be seen.

I feel myself nodding off at the cash register. Yawning, I look over at the clock. No wonder. It's almost midnight. Rail's surprise birthday poker game for Dad must've gone late. I wrap both arms around the till and close my eyes.

I stepped up my hours at Rail's store this year, ever since the railroad transferred Mike and Bill to Cumberland this past summer. Turns out Dad was right about what was going to happen when the diesels came—almost every last railroader either got transferred out of Rowlesburg or was let go altogether. Mike and Bill were two of the lucky ones, even though they hated it bad as the devil himself to move away. Now there's only a skeleton crew at the M&K—a total of less than ten men. And all of them are old and getting ready to retire. Not a man under fifty-five in the lot.

It just goes to figure that when it's finally my turn to go to work on the railroad, the durn railroad up and leaves town. And just like Dad said, there wasn't a dag-gone thing that me or anyone else could do to stop it.

Actually, Dad was even righter than he knew. Once the railroad pulled out, the cement plant up and moved right along with it. It left a heck of a lot of men out of work around here. The whole town is nothing but skin and bones compared to what it was last year. And it's left me wondering what the heck I'm going to do after I graduate high school next year. Work at Rail's the rest of my life?

I open my eyes and grab the little club I've got hidden under the cash register. Thought I heard a rustling sound outside the door, but when I look through the glass, there's nothing there. My fingers relax. It used to be I could always count on a late-night visit from Art Bishop, or Ajax or Neil. But all three of them and their families up and moved away with the railroad. Now even All Hallows' Eve is dead around here.

I look around the store, at the floor that always seems to need sweeping and the walls that could really use a fresh coat of paint. I suppose I oughta be grateful just to *have* a job in Rowlesburg these days. Heck, Rail's even offered to let me buy the store and take it over for him when I graduate next year. I feel like I oughta jump at the offer, but Dad keeps telling me not to be stupid. Rowlesburg is dying, he says. Graduating is my chance. My chance to get out of here.

But I don't want to get outta here. I just want everything to go back to the way it was.

I hear the rustling sound again—this time I'm sure of it. I tighten my grip on the club and flip my legs over the counter, knocking a peanut butter cup off the shelf and into the aisle as I land on the opposite side. I walk slowly to the glass door to have a look outside, holding the club behind my back. Another rustle.

I crane my head to look left, and out from the shadows pops Thaddeus Ore.

"*Holy Mother Mountain*, Thaddy, you about gave me a heart attack!" I say as I push open the door for him.

Thaddy's pale lips curl upward just slightly on the left, as if they can't quite remember the right way to make a smile. He pushes back greasy hair off his equally greasy forehead, his squinty eyes refusing to meet mine as they zigzag back and forth across the air before finally coming to rest on the floor. I hear him mumble something through his missing front teeth that someone who didn't know him wouldn't even recognize as a word. But it's the only thing I've ever heard Thaddy say in the store, and I've heard it so many times that my response is second nature.

"That's all right, Thaddy," I say. "Nothing to be sorry about. You just come to have a look around?"

His whole tiny body shakes up and down along with his head, and his eyes dart like frightened spiders into every crack of the floor.

"Okay, then," I say. "Have at it."

I watch as he scampers towards the back of the store like a dog that's just been let out of its cage. I know where he's heading—to the egg bin to steal two eggs. It's something he's been doing ever since he lost his job when the railroad pulled out.

I've always had a soft spot inside for Thaddy, so at first I didn't say anything about it to Rail. I felt real bad for him not getting transferred with so many of the others to Cumberland, even though I know he could never have made it on his own there. But after he'd pinched eggs four times in the span of a week, I figured I had to let Rail know what was going on. Rail got real red in the face at first—so much so that I started taking up for Thaddy right away.

"That's not it, Jimmy," Rail said, all flustered at me. "It ain't Thaddy—for Pete's sake, I'll let him take anything he wants from this store. It's them dag-blasted higher-ups at the railroad that oughta be whacked over the head. After all them years, to pull the rug out from under him like that. I swear I dunno how the boy stays alive."

Neither do I. He never steals a thing but the eggs.

I watch him over the shelves as he skits from aisle to aisle, pretending he's looking to buy some bread or beer. When he gets to the egg bin, he stands on his toes and flits his eyes in my direction, looking for all the world like a mole popping up out of his hole. I bend over to pick up the peanut butter cup off the tile, pretending not to see what he's doing. I hear the cardboard click of an egg container opening, and Thaddy begins to hum, which means he's got the eggs. The humming is tuneless, sort of a nervous buzz. It's the sound I'd imagine would come out of a ninety-pound gnat, but for some reason it makes me feel better—like he's going to be okay, at least for another day.

As I stand up again, he scurries to the front of the store, his arms hanging unnaturally straight by his sides, knuckles forward, to cover the egg he's holding in each hand. His head turns away from me, looking towards the wall as he approaches the counter. The humming gets louder the closer he gets to the door.

When he first got let go from the railroad, I'd make a

point of saying good-bye to Thaddy as he walked out the door with his eggs, just to be nice. But after I saw how bad it shook him up each time, I finally stopped and just let him walk out in peace.

I watch him as he passes the counter. Suddenly his humming breaks off like a snapped twig. His feet freeze and his head jerks towards the front door. When I look, there are two men—or are they boys?—standing in the doorway. I take a hard swallow of air. They don't look like anyone I know from Rowlesburg, but then again I can't make out their faces. They're wearing stocking masks.

The bigger one pushes open the door with a stocky shoulder. He's wearing a black and silver Kingwood letterman jacket, halfway unzipped. His hands are in his pockets.

"Trick or treat, boys," I say as I put the peanut butter cup down on the counter, making sure they see the club in my hand. "Store's closed."

"Looks like you've got yourself one customer there," growls the first. "Ain't we good enough for your store?"

He lets out a burp I can hear all the way over from where I'm standing. Thaddy starts up his humming again. The men in the masks turn their heads towards him.

I tap the club on the counter. Their heads snap back in my direction. "Store's just closed, boys. I'm gonna have to ask you to leave now."

I take a step towards them.

The one in front jams his hands harder into his pockets. I can't decide whether it's just his fists in there or something else. I stop walking, just in case. Thaddy's humming gets louder. His eyes flit in my direction.

The front man looks back over at Thaddy. "Shut up, moron!"

I look over, praying that he can.

But Thaddy's humming gets even louder. His eyes are zipping at double speed in every direction.

The man stomps forward towards him. "I said shut up, moron!"

He shoves Thaddy back by the shoulders. It's not a particularly hard shove, but Thaddy's so light, it sends him sprawling. His head slams on the floor with a pop, like a dropped watermelon against the tile. For a moment he lies motionless except for the broken egg yolks that seep their way through his fingers onto the floor.

The man stands there looking down at Thaddy, his big hands hanging by his side. The rage in my chest twists up like a cyclone. I wind the club up like a baseball bat, and smack it hard across the bridge of the guy's nose. He flies headlong straight into his buddy. The both of them crash down under the exit sign, knocking over a display of salted nuts.

I rush him again. "You sons of . . . !" I yell. "I'm gonna kill the both of you!"

Without warning Thaddy lets out a piercing scream.

A second later the midnight train blows its horn several miles outside of town. I turn to look at Thaddy, and for all the world it seems like there's no train at all; there's a whistle been buried deep in Thaddy's chest all these years, and it's finally blowing—screaming—out his gaping mouth.

At least he's still breathing.

The horn dies away and the silence is filled up by the pond of blood I see beginning to stretch out under Thaddy's head, filling in the cracks in the tile. Out the corner of my eye I see the two men scrambling through the front door. Every muscle in my legs tightens, wanting to run after them, but I rush over to Thaddy instead.

The blood is just pouring out the back of his head. His back is arched high as the Tray Run Bridge. His eyes flutter like bird wings up at the ceiling.

"Hang in there, Thaddy," I say, rushing over to grab my jacket from behind the counter. By the time I get back to him, his eyes are closed, his back relaxed. I bunch my coat up fast and put it under his head to try to quell the bleeding.

"God, Thaddy." I put my hand on his shoulder. "I gotta get help."

He doesn't move.

I run to the door and look back. He's so daggone small.

"I'll be right back, Thaddy. You hear me? You're gonna be okay. You just sit tight 'til I get back."

I rush out the door and blaze around the corner, and in ten seconds my feet are pounding up the porch steps and through my own kitchen door. I bust into the dining room. Dad, Rail, Heevie and Uncle Clarence look up at me from their poker game.

Dad takes one look at me and gets to his feet. "What is it, boy?"

"Two men in masks came into the store an' about killed Thaddy Ore!"

The rest of the men shove their chairs away from the table.

"Holy God," Dad says. "Where is he?"

"On the floor of the store, bleedin' bad from the head."

"Let's go," says Dad, already halfway through the door.

We send Amos flying off the porch as we pound down the steps and into the alley.

"I'll run and get Doc Arnley," says Uncle Clarence, peeling off in the other direction.

Dad wheezes as he runs beside Heevie and Rail. I put it in high gear and beat them all to the store by a good fifteen yards. As I push through the blood-speckled door, I stop short on the threshold.

Thaddy's gone.

The rest of them come puffing up behind me.

"He was right there!" I say, pointing to the pool of blood. "If those boys came back and dragged him out, I'll—"

But Heevie cuts me off. "Blood ain't smeared the right way for that."

He studies the floor, walking in a wide arc over to where Thaddy'd been lying.

"See them drops of blood?" He follows a path of droplets straight back to the door. "Thaddy walked hisself outta here." He looks up at us. "Prob'ly headin' back to his boxcar."

"I dunno," I say, looking at the bloody floor. "He wasn't in any kind of shape to walk anywhere when I left him here."

We look and see that the path of blood goes right under our feet and out the door. We follow it onto the sidewalk and up the hill towards the tracks. As we step out onto the rails, the trail is swallowed by the darkness. I guess Heevie's right.

Without warning, the midnight train's horn screeches again from just beyond the river.

Our heads snap up.

This time the engineer gives several short blasts followed by one long blow.

"Oh God," I whisper. "Thaddy." I break into a dead run down the middle of the tracks towards the bridge. I gotta get to him. Now.

"Jimmy . . . !" I hear my father yell my name, but the rest of what he says is lost to the horn. It blows louder with every step I take. If I could just see around that last bend . . .

My feet pound the cross ties in rhythm with my heart, faster and faster. I clench my fists, my arms churning like the engine itself. I can see the glow of the train's headlamp right around the curve. Just another second and I'm there—

Oh God.

Oh God, no. The brakes on the train screech like a witch.

Fifty yards in front of me the train is all but over the trestle, braking for all it's worth. In its headlamp there is a shadow—a little lump lying crossways on the tracks. The train is only five yards away from it. I stop running. I can't get there in time.

The blast of the train's horn fills the town.

It's Thaddy lying there, passed out on the tracks. His neck is propped up on the left-hand rail like it was lying on a pillow.

The train screeches forward, fast as time.

"Nooooo!"

The word vaults over my teeth, mixing with the tears and spit that roll down my chin as the train sucks Thaddy under its apron, into its blackness. The engine's churning reverberates through the rails into the cross tie beneath me. Up my legs. Into my gut.

And then there is nothing.

Nothing except the train and me.

And one of us is gonna lose.

I stand my ground. The ground of every single one of my ancestors.

"Come and get me, you traitor!" I yell.

The train is only twenty yards away from me now. My chest swells up. I raise my hands.

"I'm . . . not . . . moving . . ."

I feel the engine's heat on my chest. The hit comes, but not from the front. It's from behind—a slantways blow to the small of my back. I open my eyes, flying through the air God-knows-which-way, sparks screaming past my head. My arms are pinned to my sides in a rib-crushing bear hug. My body tumbles and scrapes over the gravel, then rolls through wet grass before the back of my head smashes up against a . . .

When I come to, the wheels of the train are still screeching to a stop on the tracks. The back of my head is throbbing. I'm afraid to open my eyes. Afraid of finding slices of me scattered between the rails.

I open them anyway. There, five inches from the tip

of my nose, is my father's face. The lines around his eyes and mouth are deep as the Cheat. He grabs my aching head off the ground and pulls it to his chest. My ear is pressed to his shirt. His heart is pounding, and he's wheezing hard. Or is he crying?

"You crazy dagburn kid," he gasps, rocking me slowly back and forth in his arms. He pulls my face to his warm cheek, my eyes gazing out sideways at the train just a few feet away from us. The engine is only now coming to a stop.

It's a diesel.

My father outran a durn diesel.

THE SOCIETY

ALL HALLOWS' EVE 1949

Mom has a stranglehold of a hug around my neck, like she's never gonna let me go. Her nose is burrowed down deep into the collar of my shirt, her wet sobs oozing right through the fabric onto my skin. It's just past midnight and I've got my arms wrapped tight around her on the threshold of Aunt Mary's door. I give it an off-balance knock with the toe of my boot, trying to keep Mom steady on her feet at the same time. Mary finally opens it, still tying the belt of her pink robe around her waist. I look over Mom's head at her. My eyes are wide. I have no idea what to do.

Thank God Mary does. She reaches over to Mom, laying her hand on the sleeve of Mom's black dress.

"Come inside, Mary Etta," she says softly. "You stay here with me tonight."

Mom doesn't move. She just shakes her head side to side, sobbing.

"But he'll be alone . . ."

"No, honey, he won't be alone." Aunt Mary looks at me with her eyebrows raised. "Jimmy'll be there with him. Won't you, Jimmy?"

She nods at me to say something, so I do.

"Sure, Mom." I hesitate for a second, caught like a bug in the lamplight of Aunt Mary's eyes. "You go on with Aunt Mary. I'll stay with Dad."

My stomach tightens into a knot, squeezing the truth up out of it like acid into my throat:

Dad is dead. The pneumonia finally got him.

The wake was tonight. The whole town was at the house paying their last respects. Mom did just fine through the whole thing, even after everyone left. Even after Mike and Bill got called back to Cumberland on some emergency with the railroad. Even after they kissed her on the cheek and walked out the door saying they'd get back in plenty of time for the funeral tomorrow.

Then it was just me and Mom. And Dad, of course. And then, the clock struck midnight—All Hallows' Eve. That's when it all changed. Mom took Dad's hand in hers and pressed his wedding band hard up to her lips.

"Happy birthday, William Patrick," she whispered, leaning over into the casket to kiss his face.

When she stood upright again, she let go of his hand

and fell sobbing into my arms. She was near hysterical, and I was beside myself, not knowing what the heck to do. That's when I finally decided to walk her down the street—here, to Aunt Mary's.

And now she's pulling her face out of my collar, still sobbing, looking up at me.

"You will?" she says. "You'll stay with him?"

" 'Course I will, Mom."

"All night?"

"All night."

Mom's jaw loosens a little. Aunt Mary opens her arms and Mom walks into them, sucking in sharp breaths of air as they pass together through the doorway.

"I know, honey," Mary says as she turns to close the door. She blows a quick kiss at me through the crack. And then she shuts it.

I stand perfectly still. The door's only a few inches from my eyes. I can still feel the weight of its closing on my face.

I wipe Mom's tears off my neck and fight the urge to walk by Rail's store on the way home. I still haven't given him an answer on whether I'll take it over from him or not, even though I've thought about it every daggone day since I graduated in June. I keep thinking that if I do, maybe I could make some kind of a living here. If I do, maybe things will stop changing.

A steam train whistle echoes through the foggy mountains, hollow in my ears. Sounds like it's a million miles away. It might as well be. My boots feel heavy on my feet as I trudge up to the house. The porch steps creak under their weight as I climb them. Amos is nowhere to be seen. Come to think of it, I've not seen him since Dad died.

I walk inside and pull the chain to turn on the kitchen light. The bulb flashes bright and fast, then crackles out with a pop. I feel my way towards the dining room, taking slow, sliding steps so as not to trip. The last thing I need is to knock Dad's casket over and have his stiff, cold body go sprawling out all over the floor on All Hallows' Eve. My stomach flips at the thought of it.

I take another step towards the casket. And with no warning at all the question comes shrieking into my head:

Is Dad a ghost now?

I try to wish the thought away, but the chills have already shot down my neck.

I'm at the threshold of the dining room door, and I swear I hear wheezing coming from the casket. I hold my breath and tell myself it's all just in my imagination. But the wheezing gets louder. Prickles run like voltage around my back and into my chest. There's a rustling, and this time I'm sure it's coming from the casket, not my head. My heart is thrashing like a shot dog inside me.

I stand paralyzed in the doorway, afraid to take another step. The wheezing continues, only it sounds less like wheezing and more like something inhuman. Something that's bearing its fangs, rearing its head back, ready to strike.

I lunge for the switch. Light pours into the casket.

And there is Amos, sitting black as death on my father's chest. He's hissing at me.

I sink down into one of the dining room chairs.

"Holy mackerel, Amos," I yell at him.

I start to my feet again, fixing to swat him out of the casket. But at the last minute I change my mind and sink back down in my chair. He's probably feeling just as crappy as I am. What's he gonna do now that Dad's not around anymore?

Dad's lying there with one hand on his belt buckle, the other one just off to the side, where Mom let it go when she started her crying. My eyes travel up his chest, over Amos, to his face. There's no crinkle behind his eyes. There's not a durn thing there anymore. Nothing.

My head falls into my hands.

Everything's gone. First the railroad. Now my father. Everything I ever wanted to do. Everything I ever wanted to be.

I hear Amos kneading around on my father's chest. For Mom's sake I know I ought to swat him off. But then I hear it. And I can't believe my ears.

Amos is purring.

“Dagburn cat,” I say, shaking my head. And I leave him right where he is.

My eyes close, feeling heavy beyond measure. I’m so durn tired.

I think about going upstairs to my bed, but I promised Mom I’d stay with Dad, and I figure that means *with* him. I get up to turn out the light, but then think better of it. Sleeping by a dead body is one thing. Doing it in the dark is another thing altogether.

I sit back down and pull up a second chair to prop my feet on. In spite of the light, I’m asleep almost instantly.

I must’ve been sleeping hard, because it takes a while for me to realize that the buzzing noise in my ears is Amos. He’s hissing again. I open my eyes and start to tell him to hush when I realize it’s completely dark. Someone’s cut off the light.

I hear a rustling sound, but this time it’s not coming from the casket in front of me. It’s behind my back, coming from the kitchen. And this time it’s not cat-sized. I hear the scraping of a match followed by the smell of sulfur and the scuffle of feet. The glow of a candle illuminates the room, suddenly making it look like everything’s underwater.

Slowly, I turn around. There, filing into the dining room, is Heevie Marauder, carrying a candle. He nods at me as he passes, like it's the most natural thing in the world for him to be walking into our dining room at God-knows-what-o'clock in the morning.

Rail comes in next, bottle of whiskey in hand, followed by Uncle Clarence, and Bill. Mike walks in last. He's carrying an old, brown leather book. I rub my eyes.

"Mornin', Jimmy," Rail says after they're all finally in the room. Amos hisses at him and jumps off Dad's chest, onto the floor. "Mornin' to you, too, Amos."

We all stare at each other for a second before Rail starts in again.

"I guess you're wonderin' what we're doin' here so early," he says.

"You come to pay your respects to Dad one last time?" I ask.

"Actually, Jimmy," Rail says, "first we came to see you."

I shoot a look at him. "Me?"

"Yeah," Rail says. "You."

I stare at them blankly for a few seconds. "What the heck for?"

Bill gives a little snort that I swear sounds just like Dad. "Don't you get it yet, Runt?" he says. "We're here to induct you into The Society."

I drop back down into my chair.

Uncle Clarence clears his throat. "Michael, bring me The Book."

Mike brings The Book out from under his arm and

goes over to Clarence, holding it up for him like an altar boy. It's large, both in height and thickness, and bound in leather like a Bible but without any title or lettering on the front. I recognize it immediately from Uncle Dick's wake.

Clarence flips through the pages for a minute, then clears his throat.

"Jimmy," he says, "before a man agrees to join any kind of organization, he needs to know exactly what the heck it is he's joining. You agree?"

I nod.

He cocks his head at me like he sometimes does in school when he's getting ready to ask a student a question.

"You know what The Society is?"

I look back at him. "Yeah," I say. Of course I know what The Society is. I've only been chasing around behind it my whole entire life.

Clarence looks at me with his eyebrows up, like he's waiting for me to explain the whole thing to him. Suddenly, I'm not so sure.

"It's . . ." I look over at Heevie and Rail, then Uncle Clarence and my brothers. I start to mumble something about hunting season and railroad ties, but the words don't seem to make any sense when I go to say them out loud. I stop and try again.

"Well, it's . . ." This time my memories of Uncle Dick's

wake come tripping up to a stop behind my tongue. What the heck *is* The Society, anyway? In my head it's all jumbled up together with whiskey and trains and secrets and death.

I don't know what to say.

But the beating in my chest tells me where to look.

Slowly, I get up and face my father. His white shirt is all bunched up around his chin, like a messy bedsheet that someone's been sleeping on. Amos.

Suddenly, I realize it. The Society has always meant one thing to me, and one thing only.

My father.

I turn back to Clarence, my answer to his question stuck somewhere down deep in my throat.

But somehow he knows.

"It's all of us, Jimmy," he says. "But it's more than that, too."

He looks over at Mike. "Show him."

Mike turns and steps towards me, holding out the open book.

I look down at the yellowed parchment page. On it, written in beautiful, flowing script are four names, each one written just below the other—Fineas, Ira, Elias and William—all with the surname O'Cannon. On the left by each name is a bloody brown thumbprint.

"This Society," Clarence continues, "was started nearly one hundred years ago by your great-grandfather

Patrick Fineas O'Cannon. That's his name up at the top of that page there. They called him Finney. He was thirteen years old when both his parents starved to death in Ireland, trying to keep him and his three younger brothers alive during the great potato famine. Those are his brothers' names underneath his."

I read the names again. Fineas, Ira, Elias, William.

"Those were hard times in Ireland, Jimmy," says Clarence. "No food, no jobs. Their relatives were planning on splitting the boys up, with Finney going to a workhouse and his brothers going to live in a couple of different orphanages.

"But the brothers vowed to each other that they'd stay together. They cut their thumbs and swore a blood oath that they would die rather than be separated."

I study the thumbprints. It's hard for me to believe they're almost a hundred years old. I can make out every ridge in every last one of them.

"So they stowed away in the hold of a coffin ship headed for America. But all four of them caught the typhus fever, and the three youngest boys died on board. Finney wanted to die there with them. But while he was lying there full of fever, something happened."

Clarence lowers his voice to almost a whisper. "That something is the reason you're alive today, Jimmy."

I look at him. The reason I'm alive today? "What? What happened?"

"I'll read it to you from The Book, Jimmy," he says. "In Finney's own words."

Mike brings The Book over to Clarence, who puts on his black-rimmed glasses and begins to read. I can almost hear the Irish accent as he speaks.

I lay on that ship, wanting to die, grievin' how me parents and brothers had given their lives for naught. Suddenly a flash o' light pierced the middle o' me fevered head like a hot iron. And I heard me father's boomin' voice:

"Don't go a-chasin' after the souls o' the dead, Finney, for we're nearer than you might believe. And don't go a-dyin' on this ship, either, but live. Fer it's what you do with your life that'll give meaning where it now seems like there is none. Do fer others what you wish you could still do fer us. And you'll be doin' it fer us, son. You will be."

So I swore to me father's ghost that I would do as he said. And I'd no sooner made the promise than me fever broke, the light vanished and the ship docked safe in the New York City harbor.

As I made me way along the rails, I'd think of me promise and sometimes I'd do a little something for a feller I didn't really know; and I'd get it in me head that I was doing it for me family. And it let me sleep at night.

Then one day me best pal Earl McGorry's wife and baby died in childbirth. Earl wanted to give up and die, too. So I told him the whole story of me promise to me father.

When I was done, Earl asked to see The Book. He took it in his hands and cradled it like he was holdin' his own dear baby, saying, "Finney, I swear to you this night on the souls of me dead wife and child that I will do the same." So we tipped the bottle and I cut his thumb, and he smudged his blood on the page opposite mine and me brothers.

So began The Society.

Clarence stops reading and flips again through The Book, opening it to yet another page. Mike brings it back over to me, this time holding it out for me to take.

When The Book hits my hands, the blood tingles in my fingers. There's a whole page of thumbprints in front of me. I read the top one: Earl Dunleavy McGorry. The thumbprint beside his name is heavy and smeared. Below it are nine other thumbprints, each with a name I don't recognize beside it.

I turn the page. There's another ten thumbprints beside another ten names. I turn the page again and there are more. Some of the names I recognize—Cannons, Marauders. They go on and on—there's gotta be close to seventy of them.

I flip on until I find my father's name. William Patrick Cannon. The thumbprint is clear and jumps right out at me from the rest. I touch it and take a deep breath. Then I flip through to the last print. Beside it is Mike's name. Below it is written my own.

James Grinnan Cannon.

I hold out my thumb.

Mike takes The Book and Heevie walks over to me, pulling his pocketknife out of his pants. He gives me a half smile, flicks it open, then takes my thumb and slices it down the center.

I don't even flinch.

"Gotta be deep enough to leave a scar," he says.

I look at the cut, at the blood coming out, and think of all the men who have done this before me. My father stood in front of this book, bleeding from his own thumb once.

Heevie folds his knife and hands me a handkerchief.

"Wipe off the first blood," he says. "You get too much and it smears."

I wipe off my thumb and watch the blood slowly reappear from the slit.

Mike holds The Book open. I press my thumb into it, just below his. When I peel my skin off the page, the print is scarlet—bright and fresh next to the others that are so brown.

I take one last look at my thumb before wrapping it

back up in the handkerchief. The slice is perfectly straight. It will make a good scar.

Mike blows on my thumbprint and closes The Book, holding it in front of his chest, like the priest at Mass.

"Jimmy," says Clarence, "this book contains the blood of every man who has ever been a member of The Society. You are now its bearer."

Mike hands me The Book. I take it.

We stand there for a minute looking at each other. Then Heevie walks up to my father's casket.

"The Lord giveth. The Lord taketh away. *Benedìctus Deus in Sàecula.*"

"*Benedìctus Deus in Sàecula,*" I hear my own voice boom as I step into the circle around Dad's coffin. *Blessed be God, forever.*

Uncle Clarence motions me to hold up The Book so he can flip through the pages again. He finds what he's looking for and points at it with his finger.

"You read it, Jimmy."

I take a deep breath and begin.

"'None of us lives to himself,'" I say. "'And none of us dies to himself.'" My throat narrows so I can hardly get the rest of the words out. "'For if we live, we live for the Lord, and if we die, we die for the Lord.'"

I look down at my father in the casket. His left hand is still lying slightly off to the side from when Mom kissed it and let it go. I can see the scar on his thumb. I press my own bandaged thumb into The Book as I begin to read again.

"'Do not weep,'" I say, even though my own eyes are strongly considering it, "'for I shall be more useful to you after my death, and I shall help you then more effectively than during my life.'"

But how can he ever help me now? My chest tightens. I look down at Dad's face. Panic hits me like a backhand.

My God, I'll never see him again.

Now Uncle Clarence is saying something, but I can't get myself to focus. He's positioning The Book flat in my hands, sprinkling snuff out onto the cover.

The others take a pinch of it, so I follow suit. The snuff rubs raw and spicy in the pocket of my lip, and I close my eyes for a second, trying to settle myself. When I open them again, Clarence is blowing the rest of the snuff off The Book's cover onto Dad.

The spice floats as if in slow motion out from The Book in a little cloud over the casket. I want it to stay hanging there. To freeze the night in place. To stop the casket from closing. To let him stay here with me forever.

But the snuff settles anyway.

"I remember W. P.," Clarence begins. And the stories fly out, like so many pieces of a puzzle tossed into the air. The rent he paid on Aunt Mary's house after Uncle Dick died. The railroad land he let the town use for the Victory

Gardens during the war. The night we helped him run that new boxcar off the rails for Thaddy Ore. The way he paid Thaddy out of his own salary after the railroad pulled out last year.

I never knew all *that.*

The circle has come around to me. I clutch The Book to my chest. I want so bad to tell stories like Bill and Mike about how me and Dad worked together on the railroad. How we joked around and did important things. How I learned to fix the steam engines. How he thought I was the best durn machinist the railroad had ever seen.

But these aren't my stories.

Bill puts his hand on my shoulder. "It's okay, Jimmy," he whispers. "Help me here. It's time for his last drink."

His last drink. And then the casket will be closed. Forever.

The panic flies again like bat wings in my chest as I set down The Book and put a hand behind Dad's neck. His body is cold, but his white hair is clean and soft under my fingers.

Dad's head is level with mine now, but the candlelight is playing tricks on me. The more I look at him, the less I see anything that resembles my father. I close my eyes, blinking out the wetness to help me see better. But when I open them again, I break into a cold sweat. I don't recognize this man I'm holding at all.

I gulp at the air as the whiskey begins its way in silent

toasts around the circle. They each hold up the bottle and tip it to Dad. But I can't even recognize his face. I curl my fingers tight into his shirt. My God, if I can't even recognize him now, how will I ever remember him when he's buried?

I pull him closer . . .

Then suddenly the candle flickers and it's Dad again.

I tense up at the sight, working in a fury to memorize his face before it's gone for good. Quickly, I force my eyes to trace the exact shape of his nose, the patterns of the creases around his eyes. Please, God. When they close the casket, please help me remember him. Because I feel myself forgetting.

I pull him even closer, his cold cheek now pressing up against my warm one. I breathe in deep, sucking in the smell of railroad oil that still hangs on his skin. And I close my eyes.

"Dad . . . ," I whisper.

But I don't know what to say to him. I never knew what to say.

In a moment, Bill's hand is on my shoulder again. I open my eyes. He's holding the bottle out to me. I put it slowly to my lips, and the whiskey pours like hourglass sand down my throat. When it's all but gone, I pull the bottle away from my mouth, saving the last little bit for Dad.

Bill tips Dad's head back slightly, so that his mouth opens. I put the bottle to Dad's lips and tip it high into the air. When I bring it down, the whiskey is gone.

We lay him back down in the casket. Bill and Mike reach up to close the lid. As it comes down, I block it with my hand.

My arm trembles under its weight. I look down at Dad's face one last time.

Heevie puts his hand next to mine on the lid of the casket, helping support its weight.

"It's time, Jimmy," he whispers. "Let him go."

Slowly, I move my hand away, letting them close the lid.

And then he's gone.

My heart plunges downwards, chained to the heavy weight of never again. The muscles in my neck and shoulders tighten. I look at the top of Dad's casket, desperate to call up his face in my mind. But I can't. I just can't.

I close my eyes and darkness fills me completely, a void casting shadow on everything I've ever known. All my memories of him are gone. Under my breath I curse this day. This day that will take my father away. This cold durn October. This—

All Hallows' Eve.

Like a sudden wind, the stories howl through me.

Uncle Dick's wake . . . The first day of hunting season.

Behind my eyes the blackness softens; the shroud

pulls back. And from the outside edges inward, slowly, a picture begins to develop. It's fuzzy and in black and white at first, but then it slowly comes into focus.

My sophomore-year football season . . . The day he took me with him to the M&K . . .

It's my father's face. And it's not just his face now, but his whole body, too. And now there is color. And motion. And sound. And he is no longer still, but moving, walking along the tracks of a strong railroad again, on his way to the M&K Junction, Amos at his heel.

The night he pushed me out of the way of that diesel . . .

I can see him.

He's right here behind my eyes, clear as the whistle on an old Mallet engine. The rattle of his rosary beads. His hand snatching at Amos's tail. Him snorting as he tells me for the hundredth time that it's high time I left this dagburn town.

And this time, I know he's right. Because today isn't just the day of his funeral. It's his birthday, too, and it always will be. Today isn't just the end of his story. It's also the beginning of my own.

I touch my thumb, the slit that's already beginning to heal. I look over at Mike and Bill. At Uncle Clarence, and Heevie and at Rail, who's rubbing another pinch of snuff into his mouth. And I think of the cemetery where we'll bury Dad, and the town and the river and the mountains that look down on all of it; and the railroad tracks that bind them all up together like a ribbon on a package. And when I close my eyes, they're all here inside me, too, right alongside of Dad.

And I know I'll take them with me. Wherever I go.

Acknowledgments

It takes a village to write a book. My village is deep and wide and wonderful.

Thanks to The SCBWI, for all it is—and all it does—to help children's writers be the best we can be. To Kent Brown and all the Highlights Foundation folks, whose generosity and kindness are, for me, a sign of goodness in the world. To Ellen Hopkins and Suzy Williams, SCBWI RAs and authors extraordinaire, whose vision, friendship, mentoring, and Nevadan hospitality have all been gifts to me. To Walter and Katie Burke for their hospitality and Walter's excellent "technical" advice. And to Verla Kay and all the blueboarders who are always so generous with their time, talent, and encouragement. Thanks also to Michelle Green, who helped me find my voice. And to Reader X, for her friendship and excellent suggestions regarding my manuscript. And thanks to John Hankey and James Mischke, for sharing their B&O expertise with me.

Huge thanks to my editor, Patricia Lee Gauch, who

gave me the gift of herself and made my wildest career dreams come true. And thanks to Kiffin Steurer and Tamra Tuller, who helped with anything and everything I needed. And to Laura Rennert, who always answers my many, many questions and who believed in my work before there was even a whole manuscript in which to believe. To my writerbudz: Anne Marie Pace, Kathy Erskine, Julie Swanson, Kathy May, Jennifer and Erik Elvgren, Debby Prum, Andy Straka, Mary Ann Scott and Charlotte Crystal, whose suggestions concerning this book were always just right. And to Msgr. Chet Michael and Dr. Tim Short, whose wisdom and direction have helped me with the plot of my own personal story.

Thanks from the bottom of my heart to my parents, Jim and Betty Cannon, who have been there for me every day of my life, and who have shown me through example what love really is. You are my heroes. A big hug and kiss to my uncle Mike, my aunt Audrey, my uncle Dick, and my aunt Barbara, all of whom I hope to honor with this book. Thanks to my cousin Carolyn Baumgardner and her husband, Robert Sypolt, for helping me get back to Rowlesburg. And to my cousin Roger, for his great stories. Thanks also to Susan and Sonny Cowling, who provided me with food, lodging, babysitting, and encouragement during the multiple trips that were needed to write this book. And thanks to my dear friends Maureen McGorry Oswald and Lori Mohr Pedersen, for your continuing love and support through the years. And to all of my extended family—I love you.

I especially want to thank my dear daughter, Hannah, for the joy and laughter you bring me every day. And for helping me to see the world in fresh, new ways. (And also for napping really well when you were a baby so I had a little time to write this book!)

And to you, Marshall—I could write enough books to fill a whole library, and it still wouldn't even begin to touch the depth of my love for you, or the gratitude I have for our lives together. Thank you for everything, especially your wonderfully biased and unwavering support of me.

And finally, thank God! It's done!

DISCUSSION GUIDE

- In the foreword to *When the Whistle Blows*, Fran Cannon Slayton says, "Fiction has been described as 'the lie that tells the truth.'" What do you think she means by this? Find evidence within the story and the foreword to support your opinion.

- Each chapter in this novel takes place on a different All Hallows' Eve. What significance does this particular day hold for Jimmy? How does having each chapter take place on the same day, one year later, influence the storyline? Does Jimmy change from year to year? Does his father? Does their relationship? How so? Why?

- Why does Jimmy want to work on the railroad?

- Describe Jimmy's relationship with his two brothers, Bill and Mike. What is Jimmy's impression of each of them at the beginning of the novel? Do his feelings change by the end? What role do they play in each other's lives?

- How would you describe Jimmy's relationship with his father? What do they mean to each other, and how do they choose to express their feelings? At one point, Jimmy says, "I know I'll never understand that man. Even if I live to see another hundred All Hallows' Eves." Does this statement prove to be true? What happens in the story that makes Jimmy begin to look at his father differently?

- What role does Jimmy's mother play in the story?

- Who are the members of The Platoon? What does friendship mean to them? How do they show loyalty to one other throughout the story?

- Define the word "progress." How is progress represented throughout the book? Is it positive? Negative? Both?

- Mr. Evans says, "There is a little thing we in the civilized world call 'progress.'... And like it or not I am bringing it to this little hick town of yours.'" What does he mean by this? Does he succeed? Jimmy says, "As far as I'm concerned, progress is just another word for screwing things up that are perfectly fine just the way they are." Do you agree with him? How does progress touch each of the main characters?

- Jimmy's dad says, "Rules are rules." List the rules of which you can find evidence in the novel. Are rules ever broken? Why?

- What is The Society? What does it mean to Jimmy at the beginning of the novel? At the end? Why is membership so important?

- Why do you think Heevie doesn't give Jimmy's presence away when Jimmy's hiding, watching The Society barricade the doors to the school before First Day?

- Why does the football team create a ritual around Jimmy's father before every game? What does Jimmy's dad mean when he says, "I knew you boys could win the championship from the very first scrimmage. . . . You just needed someone to tell you that you couldn't." Do you agree with him?

- Why does Jimmy's father finally take him to the M&K? What do you think Jimmy's dad is hoping to prove or to show Jimmy? What are Jimmy's expectations? Does Jimmy feel the same about being a train machinist at the end of the novel as he did at the beginning?

- Discuss the character of Thaddeus Ore. What role does he play in the life of the town—if any? What happens to Jimmy the night that Thaddeus is attacked? What happens to his father?

- What do you think it would be like to live in a town that revolved around one industry like Rowlesburg revolves around the railroad? How would your life be different? The same?

- Does Jimmy decide to follow his father's and brothers' footsteps and work on the railroad? Why or why not? What finally helps him make this decision? What do you imagine Jimmy's life is like on the next All Hallows' Eve after the story ends?